CREEK WALKING

CREEK WALKING
And Other Modern Myths

Tally Johnson

FALSTAFF BOOKS
Charlotte, North Carolina

Dedicated to my wife, Rachel, as always; to my parents for their support; and to my Great-Grandparents Kimbrell for showing me the joys of living on the mill hill.

CONTENTS

Foreword...9

Modern Myths and Mad Men..............................11

Venusberg at the Beach.......................................19

Some Hunts End Better Than Others.................27

Time Heals All Wounds?....................................47

"One Man's Meat..."..61

Creek Walking...75

A Long Time Between Drinks..............................85

The Eternal Internal Monologue........................89

On the Nuptials at Kassel Klirren… 91

Ferryman, Don't Tarry.......................................111

All Souls, All Saints...119

Devil Takes a Day..131

The Confession of Cinneaus the Lazarite..........133

The Last House on the Pavement......................151

About the Author...159

FOREWORD

HOW Y'ALL DOING? YOU GOT YOUR BIG CUP OF CAFFEINE AND PILLOW JUST in case? Great, great. I do love a good road trip, don't you? Just hop in the car and go ridin'. What? Oh, no, we're not going for a drive. You drive to work every morning. You drive to see family. Driving implies a destination and a timetable. The whole thing is just way too regimented for a road trip. Nope, we're going ridin'. Just going to see what catches our eye.

See, ridin' is a Southern thing, like tea so sweet a sip can give you a toothache. Now, we can't just hop on the interstate either. Why not? Because that defeats the purpose and makes it feel like we're driving. Besides, there ain't no interstate from where we start to where we'll end up. Trust me, I've done this before. So it's two-lane blacktop and four-lane by-passes ahead.

We'll visit small Southern towns where everybody knows everybody and preteens get a cheap thrill not found in any adult magazine. We'll ride a highway in the middle of nowhere where the veil between this world and the next and the Old World and the New is as thin as Yul Brynner's hair. We'll visit an Oceanside hotel on the Redneck Riviera that just might offer you more than a place to rest your weary head, if your key works. We might just find out what the Statue of Liberty knows about true love. Heck, we could well discover if a budding May-December romance can survive an odd hobby, and more. So make sure you're good and cozy in the back seat. Buckle up and make sure you have cash for gas, and away we go. You don't have a curfew, right? Because we won't be home for supper...

Of course, if you know anything about me, you know that I know quite a bit about ghosts. Now, all these stories are fiction, and I mean it. But, well, sometimes a body has to use what the Lord gave them to make ends meet, and that's what I've done here. Some of these tales are based on myths older than your mama's cornbread recipe, and the others ain't. Those are based on true to life, honest to God ghost stories. Heck, most of the stories and the spots are about like I've told them. See if you can tell the difference. And oh, if anyone asks, tell them you're ghost gathering, since it ain't hunting if you know where they are already. Just remember not to trespass or vandalize anything.

Otherwise, I'll deny ever having met you and root for the powers-that-be to toss you under the jailhouse.

Oh, do you like old honky-tonk music? Because that's all I've got in the player.

Modern Myths and Mad Men

"Everybody claims the South has a monopoly on eccentrics and has a pet theory on why. Too much inbreeding, too little air flow in the summer, yadda yadda. But anybody with a lick of sense knows that's false. Hetty Green, the "Witch of Wall Street"? Yankee. Ignatius Donnelly, the Congressman who thought he'd found Atlantis? Yankee. Joshua Norton, the guy out in San Francisco who thought he was the Emperor of America? Yankee. So, you don't have to have a drawl to be thought of as off."

"But it helps," I said in jest, hoping to cut off the flow of invective before it hit flood tide.

My colleague in the history and political science department at Wade Hampton College in hot and steamy Georgetown, Dr. Walter Rogers, was prone to rants of varying length and intensity, but his minimum was fifteen minutes with a decibel level roughly akin to a metal band in full thrash mode.

"In fact, I'll give you a real-life example or two of how right *they* are and then you can pick up in mid-rant… as long as you let me shut the door to my office before you get all revved up again. I don't want the math department fussing at us again."

With that, I moved to my battered file cabinet and removed a faded blue folder crammed with varying sized sheets of paper in states ranging from tattered to pristine and removed a set of yellowed sheets of notebook paper.

"Sorry, I need all the help I can get. The memory is fading out like a cheap snapshot, hence the notes. Now, what was his name…oh yes, of course, Mr. Adams…here we are…"

"Listen, Dr. Joslyn—Tommy—I'm always interested in a good yarn. Hell, it's one reason why I come hang out with you between my real classes. Folklore… meh. But, what does this Adams guy have to do with my point?"

"If you'll return to your Irish coffee, all will be revealed. You know, I bet you read the last chapter of a mystery first… At any point, here we go and, first, I'll give you some background so the story makes some sense and you can see how it relates.

"I met Clarence Adams, better known to most folks as Ole Dippy, after a childhood attempt to stuff an entire can of snuff into his lower lip in Hemphill,

South Carolina, while working on my dissertation. Everyone I had talked to before said he was a never-failing source of information on the hidden history and folklore of the area, especially the tales told in the African-American communities. His account of the Eleanor Club scare from the nineteen-forties was hysterical and accurate, among other tidbits. Basically, in a town as weird as Hemphill, and I'd put it up against Arkham, Derry, or Jefferson any day, the oddball is king. And Ole Dippy fit that bill in spades, in looks and background.

"He was dark-skinned, and his features had a definite Indian cast to them with the sharp, angular jaw and the Roman nose and piercing black eyes. Even bloodshot and rheumy, he could stare through you, despite his handicap. His hair was as dark as a moonless night in the country and, if he dyed it, it was done by a Hollywood professional. He was at least seventy back then, so I'm sure he's dead by now.

"He was born near Hemphill, to the mayor of one of the outlying black communities, Woods Crossing, I think it was. However, he moved to Richmond shortly after his birth and lived there until his mid-teens. His mother, Jessica, much younger than his father, Lewis, was basically a cipher. She mainly kept house, cooked, and had children. His father was abusive in every way imaginable and paranoid where his wife's erstwhile virtue was concerned. For some reason, most of this irrational behavior was focused on Clarence. Lewis was convinced that mother and son were having a torrid affair behind his back. Now, I'm not a lawyer, but I think Ole Dippy was being truthful when he denied this accusation even with fifty years of hindsight.

"At any rate, and keep your thoughts to yourself, the last straw for Clarence came when he received a note from his father at school during the last week of his junior year in high school. The note basically stated that the dad was going to kill Clarence and his mother to put an end to their 'carrying on' that evening. In response, Clarence simply left school, went to the nearest recruiting station, and signed up with the Marines.

"One comical aside, the way he explained getting in despite being underage and not actually lying was by writing the number eighteen on two slips of paper and putting them into his shoes. *So*, he could honestly tell the sergeant he was over eighteen when asked. Anyway, I thought it was funny and clever too, so hush.

"At any rate, he was sent to Korea and trained as a sniper. As Ole Dippy told me more than once during our chats and formal interviews, the decade he was in the service was the best time of his life. While he was on leave, he decided to go to Detroit to visit some guys from his old unit and got caught up in the aftermath of a bar brawl. Despite being in dress uniform after just getting off the bus, he was trying to break up a knife fight when the cops showed up. After being caught up in the tide of fleeing witnesses and participants, he was hit by a fluke round and shot through his right foot. When the injury required three surgeries to try to repair to no avail, he was given a medical discharge from the Corps. His odd sliding limp also dated from this injury. Basically, he drug that foot behind him like a puppy out for an unwanted walk and would have to reach down, grab his thigh, and pull the leg in front. Made any stroll seem like walking with Moses in Sinai, regardless how long or short it was.

"On his way back home to Richmond from Detroit, his bad luck kept pace. He decided to spend a layover while waiting for his next bus in Pittsburgh at a nearby tavern and got into an altercation with an older fellow. The chat ended with the older man on the floor with a shattered beer bottle for a pillow. According to Ole Dippy, the guy lived, and that was all he had to say. However, a bit of Googling and a well-placed phone call to the local library soon gave me the straight dope. The man Clarence had assaulted was 'Lousy Louie' Austin, the then-king of the Baltimore and DC policy racket, according to the *Pittsburgh Courier* accounts. He died of his injuries, but all Ole Dippy was charged with was assault and battery, drunk and disorderly, and littering. He served ninety days in jail after pleading self-defense.

"The older man had supposedly claimed to be Clarence's daddy and offered to spank him with his handy baseball bat after a political argument. The bat was not found at the scene, but Lousy Louie did have a straight razor in his sock and a loaded and unregistered pistol in his jacket pocket, giving credence to Clarence's claims. At any rate, upon his release, he decided not to return to Richmond, fearing that his presence might put his mother in jeopardy since he had not heard from his family since his hasty exit.

"He vaguely recalled having at least one living relative in Hemphill, a maiden aunt of his mother's named Mary Perry, the wife of her brother, Pauley. He tracked down her address and asked if he could stay with her, and, of course, she said yes. After a few months, he met an older widow named, with God as my witness, and I saw the gravestone myself, Jezebel. They got married and lived happily for about twenty years and had four kids—two girls named Ismene and Antoinette and two boys named Eddie and Peter. Oddly, both sets were twins.

"The boys had a rather heated sibling rivalry that bordered on pathological, but the girls were as thick as thieves. The reason for the end of this domestic bliss varied depending on who you asked. Ole Dippy simply said that it was fate and would offer no further explanation, even when plied with booze. I know it was unethical, but I didn't use it in the dissertation, so hush. Local gossip and hearsay rumor was that husband and wife had a huge fight; the children, who were home for Sunday dinner, intervened; and Ole Dippy killed them all with a pistol in cold blood, literally blind with rage.

"Ismene, the eldest by all of two minutes, found the carnage after dropping her husband, Chester, off at work at the Democrat Spinning Mill. Yes, the same one that made 'Yellow Dog Yarn, made by Democrats, for Democrats, at the Democrat Mill.' What can I say? The South of fifty years ago was a far different place than the one we have now.

"The coroner found that Jezebel and the kids had died by reason of misadventure caused by alcohol overdose. According to this version, Ole Dippy had been blinded by some homemade 'corn likker' and shot his family by firing at random in his rage. My personal belief matches what Clarence's son-in-law, Chester, told me my last night in town over a bucket of beers.

He told me that his in-laws had been arguing about 'Lousy Louie's' death in Pittsburgh all those years ago after Jezzy—a family nickname—had found a shoebox full of articles and documents about the case in the back of Clarence's closet while she was swapping out mothball dispensers. She claimed to have known 'Lousy Louie' in Pittsburgh, as well as a man named Lewis Adams in Richmond. She even said that the men were the same person and that she had slept with both of them enough to know.

"Well, you can guess how this affected Ole Dippy's mindset. Hell, if I thought I had killed my dad and then slept with my mama... hum, baby.

"Now, Jezzy wasn't exactly a braggart about her past before she met Clarence. In fact, not even her family knew much of her background, so there's no real way to prove that speculation. At any rate, Ole Dippy snapped like a dry twig in a forest fire, grabbed his pistol from its hiding place next to the stove, and started shooting. Chester said the kids were killed as they came running into the house from talking on the porch and enjoying the night breeze. Hell, if Ismene hadn't pulled up to the back door to bring groceries in and grabbed the burnt-out fluorescent tube off the back stoop, he might have killed her, too. As it was, she had time enough to bash him in the face with the tube, and the tiny shards cut his eyes up like a grape in a blender on puree. Of course, the fact that the gun was empty kind of evened up the odds some, too.

"After a quick hearing, Ole Dippy was found to be insane and sent to the State Hospital. After about ten years of primal screams, electroshock, and some other less-enlightened treatments, he was released to the tender care of his surviving daughter and her husband. To Ismene's credit, she did petition for his release, if you call being released into an unfinished room slapped on the back of a singlewide trailer with only an outside spigot, a hotplate, an air mattress, and an outhouse an upgrade from a modern mental hospital. Not to mention having to beg your own flesh and blood for your own retirement money. Now, despite all his troubles, he was a hell of a source, even if some of his better stories relied on Shadow People for any kind of verification.

"Now I'll lay you better odds than you'll find in Vegas that there are more Ole Dippies in small towns, mill hills, and railroad hamlets from Texas to Virginia than there are in all of Manhattan or anywhere else north of the Potomac!"

And after that stirring peroration to a hell of a tale, I glanced at my erstwhile colleague in plumbing the depths of the past for a sign of disagreement or a snort of fury. Instead, I saw his slumped form with his head on his chest, snoring like an overloaded freight train tackling the Saluda Grade. I kicked the sneaker-clad foot dangling limply over his knee and said, "Your turn, counselor."

With a gasp and snort, Dr. Rogers returned from the land of nod and cast his basilisk gaze in my direction.

"If you were one of my students…"

"I'd make an A," I retorted. "Now, do you even remember our discussion?"

"Yep, and despite the hard-knock life your buddy in Hemphill had, let me prove to you why the Yankees have the market covered on weirdoes," said Dr. Rogers with a subtle hint of smartassery unbecoming to his advanced age.

"I met Terry Beaumont just after graduation from college in the early seventies. Due to my own screwing around, I had applied to grad school too late to get my student deferment approved and got myself drafted into this man's army. Me, the founder of the WHC chapter of the SDS—that's the Students for a Democratic Society to the young'uns like you—drafted and sent to Fort Jackson for basic. It was an anti-war group, more or less. At any rate, I was in for a year, and I decided that since I wasn't nursing a death wish, I'd better remember some Boy Scout training and pay attention. And since I was a classic nerd in looks, I figured I had better make friends with the nearest vet real quick.

"Thankfully, one of the guys in my barracks had already put a year in the Navy and decided that being seasick twenty-four-seven sucked, so he joined the Army. He was in as a PFC and was six-three, two hundred plus, all muscle and no BS. He was an ideal companion for a coward who wanted to go study century-old state senate races and wanted to live for the next eleven months or so.

"Terry pronounced his last name as *Boo*-mont and was from Terrytown, Nebraska, which was then a village of less than five hundred people that's now a suburb of Scottsbluff. To shorten this tale, especially after you talked the plants dead with yours, Dr. Joslyn, Terry and I became best buddies and bunk-mates through basic and after our deployment in Vietnam." Dr. Rogers always did have a way with words. Not the way I had, but few do.

"After about three months 'in-country,' we drew point on a night patrol in an area that the Viet Cong attempted to infiltrate. We would rotate off every four or five hundred yards to keep fresh eyes up front. Well, I had missed my rotation by about twenty steps when Terry screamed and froze in place like a champion playground Red Light, Green Light player. And Terry hadn't ever screamed before, even when he caught a piece of hot shrapnel on his bare forearm during a firefight a few weeks before. So, I knew this sucked major ass.

"As I got close, I saw why he had screamed and didn't blame him. He had found a Viet Cong booby trap. A set of small bamboo spikes lined up about waist high on an Oriental and packed tight in a circle the size of a baseball had caught his... well, bits. As I saw the front of his uniform pants turn from olive-green to a shade of brown I've only seen on fresh dogshit, I vomited on my boots, and radioed for a Medi-vac.

"Of course, the Cong were long gone from the area. The medic did figure out that the spikes had been dipped in some mix of cobra and Komodo dragon venom, ensuring tissue death. Well, Terry got sent home, and I served out my last six months, lived through it more or less, and headed home.

"When I got back to the States, I got a postcard from Terry asking me to come visit him up in Grand Island, where he was rehabbing. Well, I jumped at the chance for a road trip before grad school, and to see my best pal, too, and headed off on a second-hand Harley that I sold in Denver at a loss to buy a damned car after freezing in the Rockies.

"I got there and asked to see Terry Boo-mont and was told to wait. After pronouncing the name correctly, I was ushered into a small private room just off the physical therapy area, where I was greeted by a striking-looking tall woman. Or so I thought. It was Terry. Basically, the docs in Nam couldn't save his penis, but told Terry about a guy at the VA in Grand Island who could make him a real woman and get him survivor benefits *and* spousal benefits, too."

Here I must have just stared at the good Doctor Rogers like he had lobsters on his forehead. "Do what now? The VA ain't known for being that progressive NOW, much less back in the days of black and white TV. This is beginning to stink like…"

"Dr. Joslyn," he said, at a volume rivalled only by the PA system at a cheap nightclub, "shush and let the grownup talk a bit."

"Well, Terry studied on this all the way to Grand Island and asked to see the doctor when he arrived for rehab. To simplify, and hush, it's my turn, damn it, the doctor had been doing this work since Korea for guys who had met with the same fate Terry had and everything would work, except that Terry couldn't make milk.

"How the hell do I know? I'm a damned historian not a doctor, Jim! All I know is my best buddy from the Army was now known as Terri and was two months pregnant by a man named Harry, who later claimed to be the former son-in-law of Oedipus. I stood as godfather to the child over spring break that year, a beautiful, healthy baby girl named Manty. Yes, it was supposed to be Mandy, but the delivery room doctor was a quack and let Terri fill out the birth certificate while I was out keeping Harry busy and distracted at the corner bar. Painkillers tend to weaken one's spelling.

"I still hate Coors beer, even after all these years. To further shorten things— *pay attention, damn it, Tommy!*—I went off to finish my research on African American third parties in Southern politics…dry I know, but I got shortlisted for the Bancroft Prize, and it got me hired here.

"I lost touch with Terri and Manty until about nine years later. I got a letter from Manty saying that her folks were bad sick and she needed me to stay with her. I came up with a Nebraska-friendly topic for some sabbatical research—I think it was the role of the Farmer-Labor movement on the Non-Partisan League in the state or something—and took off for Lincoln.

"When I got there, I found Harry had bolted with most of the checking account, Manty was keeping house by herself about how you'd expect a ten-year-old would, and Terri was in the hospital getting ready to have surgery. I grabbed up Manty and headed over there to find out what was up. I said I was Manty's uncle and Terri's little brother so they'd let me see her, and it worked. Of course, Terri's floor was limited to adults, so Manty entertained the nurses while I caught up on what was what.

"Terri said that she had found a doctor who could undo the previous surgery and old damage and scar tissue and make her a fully-functioning *him* again. She asked me to explain it to Manty because Terri's pen pal girlfriend, Clarice, was moving to Lincoln from Missoula, Montana, to consummate their year-long relationship that summer... and it was already mid-March. Hence the rushed surgery.

"She said that Harry found out about Clarice and the planned change back, freaked out, and left her and Manty broke and alone. I, of course, offered to help out, as much as an associate professor at a small private college could—being a bachelor does have some advantages—and to stay until Clarice arrived. And I did.

"Now, Terry and Clarice are married with a son named Everett, and Manty is married and has a son named Maurice. She works as a psychic reader in Aspen, and Terry is a hunting guide and amateur shaman in Missoula. Manty's husband, Randall, passed away of MRSA a few years back.

"Now, Terry's written more books than I have just about his life and has been on two different reality shows. I say unto you, my point is proven... Yankees are crazier than us Southerners any day!"

And after that whopper, Dr. Rogers slammed his half-drank jelly jar of whiskey onto the only bare spot on my cluttered desk and stalked off to terrorize an auditorium full of freshmen with the joys of the Industrial Revolution in merry old England. I made a mental note to make him pay for the next bottle or two. Lies like that had to pay for themselves. Besides, my tale was a true as the Gospels themselves, if better told.

After I finished his drink and mine (daddy always said waste not, want not), I returned to my introduction for the re-issue of Frazer's *The Golden Bough* by the National Folklore Society and thanked Heaven that I only scheduled to teach classes on Tuesday, Wednesday, and Thursday and that it was looking like a good Friday so far. I glanced at my watch and decided to cut office hours short, unless the pretty blonde graduate assistant wandered over. I'd make her translate the stack of Gullah ghost stories on my desk into something like English so I could try to track them down. But I was open to suggestions as always.

VENUSBERG AT THE BEACH

"**WELL, SHIT, ANOTHER NIGHT WASTED IN THE PURSUIT.**" TIM JACKLIN SIGHED as he handed the cabbie a twenty he thought was a five, not that the flickering streetlight offered much help in identifying the bill. "And back to 'Piss Off the Porch' to boot. Fucking yay. My own little slice off Heaven's ass."

A word about "Piss off the Porch." The actual name of this, to quote the brochure, "fine family ocean-side resort," is Pizzaro's Porch.

It harkened back to the days when every mom and pop motor lodge on the Grand Strand had to have a hook of some kind. For about three minutes in the late fifties, conquistador chic took hold. Cortez, Balboa, and their bloodthirsty friends and pointy metal helmets showed up everywhere. The couple that had just opened the Pizzaro had toyed with names from the coast's rich plantation heritage and even its recent military onslaught, but decided that Spanish tile and garish shades of pink, green, and blue would do as well.

The nickname came from the thousands of spring breakers and senior weekers who stayed there and chased everything with breasts and drank cheap beer by the gallon...and disposed of it from any convenient spot, even off the balconies.

Sadly, despite changes in decor, tastes, and more, the couple never changed anything. Hell, the place still had a working and stocked cigarette machine in the lobby. Chesterfield filters for four shiny quarters and an ashtray built into the counter. Every room was non-smoking, if you didn't smoke in them. However, for at least fifty years prior, everybody else had. Nothing says clean air like a noseful of a cigar from 1967 just before you pass out from oxygen deprivation. Assuming you can sleep on Day-Glo pink sheets and mattresses stuffed before WWII. Not to mention the glowing green seashells on the sky blue painted walls and the sweet sounds of a dozen spring breakers all on the tenth hour of a two-hour party crashing through the tissue-thin walls.

But the rooms were cheap...forty bucks at high season and before the twenty-five-story condo complex had been built across the street. Every room did have an ocean view and, assuming the screens had survived spring break and senior week, you could catch the sea breeze, too.

Since he had been staying there since he was able to walk across Ocean Boulevard, the place was what came to mind when one said "the beach" to him. Along with twenty-somethings in bikinis, golf courses every other mile, and hospitality night drink specials every night after eleven. *So*, that's where our erstwhile narrator was at this point. Coming back to a motel that never had a hey-day, alone at thirty-nine, stomach doing tricks that Letterman wouldn't book from the cheap booze and bar grease he'd lived on for the last ten hours, as horny as when he started the search, and just as unfulfilled as when he'd arrived three days ago.

Now, he'd stayed in room twenty-seven since he was able to drive here himself. Every year, the third week in May and the last week of July. Before that, his mom had insisted they stay on the ground floor "in case the big storm comes." Of course, now, his mom wouldn't know it if an A-Bomb fell on her home. Four or five years of annual strokes will do that to you.

His dad had met a drunk driver going one-ten the wrong way on the interstate coming home from a business meeting in Savannah about twenty years before. Just in time to wreck his high school graduation, but he wasn't bitter. Well, not until the judge tossed the case when the driver hired the local state senator as his lawyer. And two weeks later, the judge was appointed to the state supreme court. Then he got bitter. And had damned near stayed that way through three years of college until he discovered the wonder that was George Dickel over ice.

So, it cost him another year of college to make up the classes he either slept through or missed to reload. It made everything else manageable, especially when his girlfriend since junior high dumped him during her senior year because he was "slacking off." Then Mr. Dickel introduced him to his pals, Messrs. Beam, Daniels, and the Walker brothers.

He managed to coast through the rest of college and get a job, despite his love of late nights and liquid lunches. Anyway, he managed to climb the stairs to the second floor in less than ten minutes and even managed to find his room key in less than two. Sadly, the door he stopped at to find his key was room twenty-nine, not twenty-seven. And one of the ways that the couple had managed to keep maintenance costs low was to have every room keyed the same. This made duplicate keys cheap to make, and as long as their clientele managed to guess right more often than not, the refunds didn't bite the bottom line too hard. Hence, the lack of difficulty he had in opening the door to the wrong room.

He noticed nothing unusual at first. The room was as cluttered as his own and all the lights were out, except for the small dolphin-shaped nightlight in the bathroom. Only the realization that he was being watched, clinically observed even, aroused some doubt in his booze-clouded mind.

After he had finished draining his toxically over-served bladder and had clumsily washed his hands, he emerged from the bathroom to a vision better suited to a saint than a poor and purposeful sinner like himself. She was a copper-haired beauty who wore her long curly hair in a simple ponytail. Her skin was the alabaster white of a new tombstone, but as smooth as a used car salesman's patter with a blue-haired biddy. Her brown eyes shone like a streetlight on a foggy moonless night and damned near reached out and grabbed him from across the dark room. Skin and a face like hers had as much need of makeup as a paraplegic needed a jet engine.

She wore a long-sleeve white silk shirt with a button-down collar with two buttons undone, revealing the smallest clue of cleavage, just enough to trigger pleasant thoughts, but not dirty ones. If not for the subtle glow of it in the darkness, he would have thought she was wearing one of his old work shirts. He made no notice of any bra straps or any other visible signs of underwear, which brought back the results of the night's failed pursuit in grim detail.

He crossed the floor like a spaceship caught in a tractor beam, heedless of any obstacle. He felt at least one plastic bottle explode under the strain of his two-hundred-plus pounds and heard several more go sliding across the stained carpet, more than likely mere sacrifices to the queen bed's maw.

She was sitting in the overstuffed desk chair in front of the tile-covered, round wrought iron table. The black peasant poufy skirt she wore stopped just past her knees and matched the white silk blouse perfectly. Her long legs were demurely crossed at the ankles, and her feet vanished into the shadow cast by the table and chair. She smiled and patted the far end of the table, her unadorned hand holding more interest for him than a flute to a cobra in a basket.

"Have a seat, Timothy. I've fixed you a drink. Jack and ginger is your current poison, isn't it? We have a lot to discuss and only a short while for it."

He moved faster than he had in years to seize the offered barstool. It was roundish, wooden, and unpadded, but he had high hopes of being off it before it caught up to his back. With his best rakish grin, he looked into her perfect eyes and turned his charm up to eleven.

"My apologies for the unplanned intrusion, but from the looks of things, you don't seem to mind...much. I'm afraid you have me at a mild disadvantage since I'm on your turf and you know my name. Please, at least, even us on that score."

"I'm sorry, Timothy, I am...Vicky to my friends. I do hope you will consider me as such, since I feel like we've known each other forever. Now, we need to discuss this...unplanned visit."

"Ma'am, I mean, Vicky, I swear this...happy accident was just that. I thought I was returning to my lonely bed, not to this little piece of paradise. I'd offer you a beverage since talking is known to be thirsty work, but I'm a bit underprepared, as you can see."

"I'm fine, thank you. And as true as that may be, some manner of penalty must be paid since you did enter without my permission. Now, I could notify the authorities..."

"No, no. No need for that. What did you have in mind?" he asked, hoping that this astoundingly classy lady's mind ran through the same gutter his did, but having more doubts than a Democrat at a Klan rally.

"Well, we should discuss what caused this visit; I believe the last drink was...a double tequila shot? And then discuss what would be next?"

"Yes, but I don't remember seeing you on any of the planets I visited tonight. Heck, I closed Planet Hollywood with a vodka and tonic, then headed off to Krypton. Somehow, I don't think we move in the same circles. For one thing, you're my age, at the risk of adding insult to perceived injury. For another, any lady as classy as you are and dressed in that outfit would have been engulfed in humanity long before you made it to my back-corner barstool. So, I will have to simply ask you to dinner tomorrow so you can show me what I've been missing."

"Dinner sounds divine. I am in need of a good reliable guide to the area since this is my first trip... down in many years. Most of my old haunts are long gone. Heavens, the last time I was here, I stayed with a friend on Pawley's Island."

"Really? I can certainly fill *that* void, and hopefully any others, since my schedule just cleared for the rest of the week. Pawley's, huh? You are in for quite the culture shock. Who's your friend? I may know her."

"Oh, I really doubt it. She passed away some time ago after a huge fight with her oldest brother. Something about an unsuitable choice of lover or some such, like anybody has any real say in who they love. Her name was Alice."

"Mmmmm. Sounds tragic. Anyway, folks just need to mind their own business. Unless big brother wanted it for himself, he really had no say in the matter at all."

"It was a different era. It's that way in some families, especially old-moneyed ones in remote areas."

He never heard anything after "It was…" because his attention was diverted by the popping of the top two buttons of her blouse on their own. Thank the Lord for well-worn silk. The emergence of most of her ample cleavage and the dainty blossoming of her floral-print silk bra swallowed his attention like a prize bass striking a lure. The more he stared, the more obvious his distraction became. His subtle squirming begat obvious wiggles that led to his leaping off the barstool to make some much-needed "adjustments" to her obvious delight. When he sat back down, he noticed that the glasses were gone and had been replaced by a four pack of energy drinks fresh from the fridge, the condensation beading up and streaming down the sides.

"Now that we have made the small talk and shared a drink to break down any reservations, and made vaguely pleasant plans for the future, I need to ask you a very simple but vital question, especially given your… condition. Are you going to spend the night with me tonight? I'd say sleep, but we both doubt that will be the case, hence the change in refreshments."

After opening one of the cans and letting the metallic twang of too much caffeine settle on his tongue, he answered, "My my, that's a pleasant change. *I'm* the one being propositioned and much less crudely than I normally do it. Of course, you are sober, and I'm beginning to be that way. Now, somehow, I do believe that will happen, but I *am* a bit curious. Why me? I'm small town, small time white trash with a bad case of boozing and the 'bite mes.' Not to mention my middle age spread and hair in faster retreat than a Frenchman from a bar fight. Again, why me? You could and should have any male living or dead at your beck and call. *So*, before I oblige you, kindly oblige me."

"You have no real ties. Not to a place, not to a person. Not to any cause, great or small. Why, you don't even have a real axe to grind. I offer you what you say you've always wanted. A beautiful lady, willing and more than able to fulfill *all* your needs. A dame as witty and as profane as you fancy yourself to be, with the added bonus of being able to hold my liquor and being closer to you in age than your usual conquest. A woman kind enough to forgive the fact that you basically broke into her motel room, but kinky enough to proposition you in plain English. So, what's it going to be? We need to make hay while the sun shines, as the old saying goes."

She stood, having discreetly undone the required buttons and zippers while she spoke, and her clothes fell away like dead leaves in a fall breeze. Only the floral silk bra and matching panties were left. Her readiness and need were obvious, assaulting his senses like a hippie at a laser light show on good blotter acid. Her color changed; the stark paleness exchanged for the rosy pink of an azalea bud at Easter. Her crimson lips parted ever so slightly, and he could hear her breath quicken. Her nipples rose as if blasted by an arctic front, straining the thin silk almost past enduring. Her want stained the crotch of her panties and filled his nostrils from across the room.

No reply came from his mouth, which was hanging as open as his mind was at that moment. He stripped mechanically, never glancing anywhere but at the sheer perfection before him. He kicked off his beat-up loafers, sending two pennies flying in opposite directions. He heard one of them meet a bottle in mid-flight, but could not tell where it hit.

The sweat-encrusted and ripe with bar stink green polo shirt vanished under the AC unit, becoming an unwitting sponge for the dregs of his forgotten drink. His webbed belt and the plastic button of his khaki shorts went flying in opposite directions. As his thumbs slid under the waistband of his light blue boxers, the modern world intruded into this centuries-old tableau. Out of habit, but not necessity, he had set his cell phone's alarm for what he drunkenly thought was nine a.m., but was actually for three a.m. As the chipper tones of some forgotten pop song filled the air, whatever spell had been cast was as broken as a Victorian bride's hymen.

Suddenly, the suave ladies' man for all seasons was replaced by a self-conscious nerd. His error in opening the wrong room, the divine vision now lying atop the hideously garish comforter with her fingers running along her close-cropped pubes and the entirety of the night's events in between came back and drove him to an unthinkable decision.

"I'm sorry, but I have to go now," he stammered softly.

"Nooooo," she whined, her need as present in the room as them both. "Stay with me. Your need is as potent as mine. That's why this all happened. *Nothing* is accidental."

"Sorry," he whispered again, knowing he'd write the whole evening off as the result of something added to a drink by some horny and wound-up waitress the night before, assuming he didn't remember it all in all its inglorious detail and beat himself bloody with regret. He quickly grabbed the doorknob and threw it open, ignoring the fist-sized hole it punched into the innocent drywall behind him. He inhaled deeply, steeling himself to turn and close the door on that vision on the queen bed.

"*Wait!*" she said with a voice more used to command than seduction. "Let me show you what you have forsaken." With that, the mirror above the TV came to life. He saw them together in every imaginable form of embrace. They were the talk of every room they entered and the life of every party. The happiness was damn near a living thing. He flinched involuntarily as it faded back to reflecting the drab near-darkness of the room as usual.

"Well, I've never been one for good decisions, but I'll be here at six to pick you up for our dinner date." He grinned, hoping to use his limited charm to repair the breach.

"There will be no dinner. Like Adonis, like Tannhauser, you have forsaken pleasure unknown for the pains of the known. Exchanged bliss for a trifle."

With that, the room filled with a violet light brighter than the sun gone supernova. The last thing he saw before he closed his eyes was her grin of bemused disdain. The maid found him sprawled in front of the open door and called the ambulance. The EMS techs said he was basically fine, but that he might want to see a doctor about the burns around his eyes. They both agreed that they looked like his eyes had been welded shut.

SOME HUNTS END
BETTER THAN OTHERS

"DIDN'T YOU USED TO BE HANK TOLSON?"

That was the way Bob Roderick introduced himself to me on that night in late May.

I was sitting in my usual booth at the honky-tonk / truck stop / what-the-hell-ever outside Grants, New Mexico, noshing away at my usual two a.m. feast—a greasy chili-cheeseburger with extra cheese, a bottle of Pearl Beer, and a cig or six.

For those of you whose attention span was wiped out by too much MTV back in the day, I used to be somebody. Not the broke freelance delivery guy you see now. I was the studio host of a little show called *Y'all Gotta Watch This...* It aired for about three years on Spike and G4—reruns only—at midnight on Fridays. It got decent ratings until we decided to do a live ghost hunt at Dealey Plaza and the old Texas School Book Depository.

I was redneck enough to make the guys feel smart and cute enough in that grizzled Colin Ferrell sense to make the ladies tune in between clips of table dancing skinks and nut shots. I actually had some experience with the supernatural, having written a quickie bestseller about the ghosts in Eastern State and Alcatraz—among others—called *Spooks in the Slammer*.

The tone was snarky enough to interest Hollywood, and the writing was good enough to get it reviewed positively by *The Washington Post*. It ain't number one on the *Times* list, but I'll take it.

Anyway, we screwed around in Dallas trying to catch Lee Harvey's spirit getting ready to take out JFK again for two months and got fifteen minutes of shadows and odd creaks. Now, we had to fill an hour, and the weirdness was the star, so I decided to pad the atmosphere some. A little help from the prop guys and a crew member and we had a visual of Ole Lee Harvey walking to the sniper's nest and the sound of a rifle being loaded and fired. Not to mention a few moving boxes. I knew it was flimsy, but the 50th anniversary of the assassination was coming up, and we knew the ratings would spike. Hell, we had plans for three more Kennedy shows. JFK Junior at the Essex County airport in Jersey, Jackie in her old apartment, and Bobby at the Ambassador, well, what was left of it anyway. Pure gold, man.

Anyway, we filmed the bogus stuff after the real stuff, what little there was, and got rights to some archival stuff. Then, the producers fired the crew guy who had played Lee Harvey for selling pot to college kids. The guy got even by ratting us out a month before air, but after the promos had started. The network freaked the hell out. The suits started screaming about liability, loss of trust, loss of ad money, etc. I tried to con them into doing the show as a recreation, but they decided to cut their losses and cancel us. Naturally, I was blamed since it was my idea and since I was the face of the show. The DVD sales help pay for the truck, and I'm not broke, so it was cool.

Of course, Hollywood sealed me out like a Ziploc bag, so I headed for the sticks to reconnect and be myself. Hell, part of the charm of NW New Mexico was the fact that some Hollywood types had retired there, so I could stay current if I ever got the bug to head back, but it was rural enough that folks didn't give a damn about my past as long I left them alone and did what I said I would when I said I would. And hell, how I could I pass up a chance to live in a town called Thoreau?

I knew Roderick to speak, but we weren't drinking buddies. He was a bit sleazy, even by Hollywood standards, but had a rep among drivers and folks on the road as a stand up guy and honest enough, if you didn't get real curious.

Now, as a freelance delivery guy, I've done some shady stuff, but everybody knew I wouldn't do anything illegal.

Some guys would run loads of meth or weed over the border or serve as occasional coyotes. I had no interest in pissing off the Border Patrol and counted a few deputies as poker buddies, which was a big help with the speeding tickets, natch. So, I looked up and mumbled, "Yeah, I was, but I'm just me now. What ya need, slick?"

"Somebody who can drive a Suburban and work a movie camera. Youse fit that bill?" he said.

"Not at the same time, but yeah, I handle that. You getting into roadside porn now?"

"No, smartass, this job is actually up your alley and might get youse back to the bright lights. You free for the next month or so? It's a cash job, if that helps."

"Always does. So, who do I gotta kill?"

"Meet me at the office this afternoon, say about five? And I'll tell youse 'bout it".

"Okay. You in the same place?

"I surely am, my man. I surely am."

Now, Roderick's office was a running joke. He had bought one of the old unimproved rest areas off I-40 over near Thoreau from the state at an auction a few years back. He found an old silver Airstream and parked it in the middle of the lot and installed a cattle gate at the entrance. At least once a year, a rookie state trooper would report him for squatting on gummit property and wind up back working mall security. Or a hopped-up trucker would pull off to piss and take the gate out.

Rumor had it that quite a few of 'em wound up seeing Chaco Canyon up close. The trucks would wind up in the "parts for sale" ads in the local Auto Trader rag. Anyway, Roderick was known to be a freelance fixer. Rumor had it he was mobbed up back East and came West with the Witness Protection folks after ratting out a mob stoolie.

All I knew was his cash wouldn't bounce and he knew my quirks concerning the law. I figgered he wanted me to deliver some "borrowed" truck parts or other junk to a pal in need or something equally glamorous.

I headed home to my apartment, which doubled as the only used bookstore between Santa Fe and Flagstaff. Yeah, I can even read. Hell, I made enough money selling used romances and jack mags to truckers and tourists to pay the everyday bills. The delivery bit was a way to kill time and pad the bank account between royalty checks. I grabbed a few hours sleep and called my folks to check in. Hell, man, a body never knows what'll happen with such classy acquaintances.

Sure enough, I was outside Roderick's beat up cattle gate at five minutes 'til five, laying on the horn like a New York cabbie at rush hour. Some stoolie came down and let me in and gave me the most perfect "fuck you" look I'd seen since Hollywood. I parked my beat up, black Ford truck with the camper back next to a brand new red Suburban with a dash-mounted Super-8 camera that cost more than I was worth. With a low whistle, I wandered in.

Roderick was sitting behind a desk that had never been clean or new. I'd seen nicer shitters at Boy Scout camps in August. A top of the line police scanner and juiced up CB rig took up a shelf over his bald and sun-baked head. It looked like a wildcat trucker's dispatch office, if the dispatcher had fingers in everything ya could think of and insisted on wearing nylon suits from a bad 30s gangster flick in the damn desert. However, I did see an envelope with my name on it with the tips of at least ten 100 dollar bills peeking out, so he had my undivided attention.

"Howdy, Hank." He grinned. "Ready for some easy money and a bit of fun in the bargain?"

"Yeah, I guess. Now what's the big job?"

"You ever have the pleasure of driving Route 491?"

"Yup, a few times. It's out past BFE and two lanes of nuthin'. Why? You doing bidness on the Rez now?"

"You ever drive it at night?"

"A few times. Hell, I think I've driven everything from I-40 to sheep paths since I've been here. You ever gonna quit with the cryptic and spill? I know I'm not gonna be toting tourists or some shit."

"You ever use a Super-8 or did youse just look pretty in front of one?"

"Yeah, I learned during breaks at UCLA. Always figgered I'd wind up doing grunt work after the pretty wore off. I saw the sweet dash-cam. *So*, what, you gonna make a movie?"

"Nope, it was my boy's. Youse know he was going to film school before he got drafted out to Iraq. Thought about having you write him a letter, then realized it wouldn't help. I'm... borrowing it. Got a digital camcorder, too. A Handi-cam or some such."

"Okay, look, I can work a camera, but I could be out hustling some deliveries. The landlady ain't gonna take my dick in lieu of payment forever, and I'm past due like two months. So, you gonna 'plain this mess or what?"

"Youse still into the ghosts or did ya quit that too?"

"Yeah, I still dig 'em. Go out and play some when things are slow. Why, you wanna pet?"

"Youse ever heard of Route 666?"

"Yeah. I saw the *Supernatural* episode. It's out in Alabama or some shit, ain't it? Those Winchester kids are so stupid. Seeing demons everywhere."

"Umm, okay, whatever, if you say so. Hell man, Route 491 *is* Route 666. I keep forgetting you ain't a local boy. From down South to Hollywood to New Mexico... quite the world traveler, ain't ya? It was the sixth highway to branch off old Route 66 back in the forties, so they numbered it 666. The Zuni and Navajo raised such hell that Richardson got the number changed before he was Veep. "

"So? You working for the Hysterical Society now? Why should I give a shit?"

"Cos you're gonna be driving it for the next month. Every night from dawn to dusk, or say eight at night to seven in the morning anyway. A cool grand a week and a buck a mile and whatever else ya need."

"Dayum, not bad for some joyriding. But what about my regular stops? I do have folks that use me once a week or so."

"I'll take care of 'em, promise. If ya have any trouble, I'll fix it. Just let me know."

"Okay, so what's up with the film stuff, seriously?"

"Just run the dash cam every night steady. If ya stop to piss or get coffee, leave it on, but nobody wants to see it. While you're out, take the camcorder. The dash cam has a view screen on the console and should catch pictures from all directions without you worrying about it. I'm... curious. "

"I'm guessing they's a ghost since you asked about me and them. What is it? A phantom hitcher? Bad wreck replay?"

"Nah, not really, but when the shit hits, you'll know. And the shit on 666 ain't no camera tricks, I promise youse. You still willing?"

"For a grand a week, fuck yeah. And I'm not scared of damn ghosts. You forget, this ain't my first Ro-day-o, slick."

"Well, here's the plan. The Suburban is gassed up all the way in both tanks. If ya need to stop, hit either of the truck stops. The one in Newcomb closes up at midnight, but the chain one in Shiprock is open all night. Give the one in Newcomb my name, and they'll hook ya up on gas, grub, or whatever else. Now, when ya stop to grub, kill the cams. I have no interest watching ya eat or bang a lot lizard or whatever you do to stay awake. There's not a radio in the Suburban because I think your ears'll be kept busy."

"That's fine. From I remember, making sure highway hypnosis doesn't get you is half the fun. What about the speed traps? I know those County Mounties will cum buckets to snag a new Suburban and my DL ain't zactly crystal right now."

"No problem. I've got some contacts out there. You'll have a Nextel since cell service is kind of... iffy at best."

"Also known as there ain't none," I laughed. "Seriously, Bob, why me? You've got enough folks on the payroll that one of them would jump all over this, especially for a grand a week and 'spenses."

"Hank, you know bullshit from bacon with this mystic shit. I've read ya book and nothing really ever spooked ya. Hell, the show wasn't bad, and you'd call bullshit in a skinny second. Besides, my boys are all locals and that road ain't real popular after dark."

"What the hell ever. Folks just scared of local cops with a mad-on for driving while wasteds and open beer cans. Well, I better head on. It's after six, and it's an hour or so to Gallup. Oh, for this movie, or whatever it is, you want narration or not?"

"Not if it's extra. Here. Aw, hell, go ahead. It'll kill time for the first night or three. Describe the scenery or whatever I guess. Hell, when the big turf splats the fan, I doubt you'll need narration though. Oh, bring the tapes back, and I'll make ya copies. Call me at six a.m. and head back. I'll meet ya here and then you can rest up and dick at the shop for a few hours. Just be back at Gallup by, say, seven p.m. Don't speed in Cortez. Those folks are real techy about folks doing favors for friends. And, just so ya don't think one night will do for the whole gig, both cams have time/date stamps. No tape, no green."

"Natch, my friend. Now, do I get some gas money or will ya need a receipt?"

"I'll front ya a couple hundred for the first few days. Be careful."

"See ya in the morning."

And that was the way things went for the next two weeks. I managed to hit a road runner and a few four-legged coyotes, but no creepy-crawlies popped out and went "booga-booga."

I made a date with the cashier at the Flying J in Shiprock and managed to get laid for the first time in a couple of months after the second week. The tapes weren't exactly Oscar material. Mostly the arc of the hi-beams and a few overloaded semis heading toward Mexico. The occasional cactus or brush made an appearance, and the local wildlife as mentioned did pop up a few nights.

I did call the Border Patrol to check on some illegals outside Nakabito who looked like they hadn't seen water in a week. But Roderick kept the cash coming, and the Suburban drove like a dream, so it wasn't bad. I finally got curious and did some digging online and at the shop, trying to figure out what he was up to. No major crimes had occurred on old Route 666. One of the local state troopers made some rash comments about a mad trucker trying to run down folks about ten years before, but that was written off as a bored cop wanting to get his name in the paper.

The middle of the third week, I managed to track him down. He had quit the state police after his comments stirred some turds with the Navajo Tourism folks and opened a liquor store just over the Arizona line in Ganado. I called him up and told him who I was and that I was working on a new book about "Urban Legends of the Desert Southwest" and had heard his name.

Matt Rydell was his name, and he had joined the NMSP after serving as an MP in Guantanamo in the late Aughts. He never had any trouble with the bosses and was short listed to be moved to the Governor's security detail in Santa Fe when he mouthed off. I told him I had found a mention of his theory of the mad trucker in a book by some ivory-tower academic named Johnson who probably wouldn't know a ghost from a garbage bag from back East and wanted his opinion on it.

Rydell grinned and said between shots of Jack Daniels black, "I've read that book and I ain't in it. You can come clean, or I'll shut up like a whore's thighs at Mass. I've heard from a guy working the late shift on 491 that you've driving it hard for the last few weeks. I wanna know what's up or I'm done and you're back to square one with your head up your ass. And pass me those circus peanuts."

"Circus peanuts? The hell? Don't you mean the *roasted* ones?"

"Nope, I mean the circus peanuts. They help soak up the booze before my ulcers do. Now's what's the skinny?"

He dipped a circus peanut into the glass of whiskey, turning it the exact shade meant when folks talk about "baby-shit brown," then slurped it down like an oyster.

Fighting my gag reflex, I said, "Well, ain't much to tell. Bobby Roderick's got me driving 491 and filming it every night for a month. That's it. I got no real clue why, but the cash don't bounce. I found you online, read about you and this phantom trucker, and figgered I'd ask you why."

"Seen anything weird yet?" he asked as he repeated the process with the bright orange chunk of sweetened foam rubber.

"Naw, just the usual stuff that happens when ya ride backroads, but nothing old-fashioned queer yet."

"Okay, I'll tell my guess about why Roderick's so interested. But, first, whadda know about the road's history?"

"Well, it was built back in the thirties as a spur off Route 66. Two lane blacktop. Mostly semis after dark, unless the tourists get bored with the interstate and wanna see the real West or some such. Drivin's not bad, but the thing's maintained like a poor boy's car. More potholes than pavement. Little Water and Sheep Springs are speed traps, but I don't lead foot it anyway."

"Yeah, posting a cop in Sheep Springs was my baby," he giggled as the fourth drink started to bypass the ulcers. "Now, here's the reason he's so hot to see what's up on the ol' Devil's Highway, as we cops useta call her. Bobby ever mention that he had kids?"

"Yeah, he mentioned a boy in Iraq. Not sure if he's still there or not. We ain't zactly hanging out at Ruthie's sharing a bottle, ya know? I'm just a grunt out for a buck. What's his kid got to do with it?"

"Well, he had a daughter. Real pretty gal. Pale skin, but real dark eyes and hair. If I was ten years younger, I'd have chased after it myself. Nice big tits to boot. Anyhoo, about six or seven years back, she'd have been about seventeen or eighteen I guess, her and some of her girlfriends were out joyriding in her new Mustang out between Twin Lake and Buffalo Springs after midnight, 'bout this time of year, around graduation. Rowan, I think her name was, had started drinking out of Pop's private stash and was wasted and tired. She took the curve there at Tohatchi running about ninety-five, jumped the rail, and got thrown from the car. You need a map for the rest?"

"Lemme guess, she was the only fatality and didn't have her seat belt on?"

"Hell, she was the only one *hurt* a-tall. Now I think he's so interested in that dammed road cos of Nightgown Girl myself. But I will give ya one little tidbit of info that never made the police report. One of the girls said she thought an old seventies sedan was tailing 'em before the wreck. Like with brights on and all up in they trunk. She thought it might stop after the wreck but never saw the lights go pass or heard the brakes. We wrote it off as the ranting of a hysterical drunk girl trying not to blame her friend for being dumb."

"Whoa, whoa, whoa! What the fuck is a 'nightgown girl'? Have you knocked off a bottle when I wasn't lookin'? I've hunted some ghosties in my day, and that's a new one."

"Dat's right, you ain't a local boy. I keep forgettin'," he slurred as the dregs of the bottle vanished without the aid of the long-forgotten circus peanuts. "Ole Nightgown Chickie is a fixture on 666… 491… whatever it is. She's always seen on the side of the road. She's pasty pale, gots long black hair hangin' lucy-goosey, and wears a long white nightgown, ya know, the almost see-thru kind. Hee hee. Has those big ole eyes like those Jap cartoons. Anyway, she's always barefoot in any kinder weather, heat, rain, snow, whichever, and looks just pitiful. Folks always stop and pick 'er up out of pity, I reckon. Soon as the car stops, she vanishes. And then they'd call us'n to find her and calm 'em down. Never even found footprints. I almost think folks wuz as drunk as I am now."

"Hold it now, you mean she ran off, like she was jokin'?"

"Nope, dumbass, I mean vanish, like *poof*! Course, most folks round these parts think she was the victim of some wreck back in the day or one of ole Davy Parker Ray's playtoys that got missed. Hell, one old guy swore he saw her in the mad trucker's cab one night. Shortly after, he wound up drinkin' ammonia thinkin' it was vodka, so that's 'plains *his* problem. Nobody's ever seen her if they've had car trouble or have stopped to take pictures, only if they're movin'. Heck, a few folks say they've seen her in the daytime."

"So she's a phantom hitchhiker? Hell, I ain't picked one those up since college. And she's a hottie too, huh? And what the hell is a mad trucker?"

"From what I 'member 'bout spooks, which ain't much, most phantom hitchers actually get in the danged car. If they ain't, what ya call it, urban legends. Our chicky don't. Just don't have no car trouble on ole 666 and you won't hafta worry 'bout the trucker."

"Well, thanks for the help, I guess. Want me to call ya a ride 'fore I head out?" As soon as I asked, I saw he was face-down on the empty bag of circus peanuts after knocking the bowl of roasted ones all over the place. I paid up our tab and got a thermos full of coffee for the road. I'd be pushin' it to get over to Gallup by eight as it was. The waitress said she'd take care of "Ole Matty." And I left, pondering all what he had said.

I wish I could tell y'all that the shit hit the fan that night, but this is real life, not some Z-grade slasher flick. Roderick never let on that he knew I had talked to Rydell and even ponied up for the drinks. The rest of that week went okay, though I noticed a bunch of crows flying overhead. Thought it was awfully early for 'em, but whatever. I did cram another coyote, but the Suburban shrugged it off like I had flattened a beer can. Now, the middle of the last week, the wheels started coming off.

The first sign that the gig had gone south was the rain. After three weeks of clear nights and decent temps—for the desert, anyway—that Tuesday, we got a mamma-jamma of a gully washer. Must have gotten an inch an hour. I managed to gas up in Gallup and headed out, but I did notice that the right rear tire was getting bald. I decided to try to whistle up some fun since I had done all the narration I could stand and I was ready for a change of pace. I remembered what Rydell had said about "Nightgown Girl" and figgered I might get lucky.

On my second run, just outside Naschitti, I noticed a vodka bottle in the road. It was about one a.m. I managed to catch it with the bad tire, and it went down like a boxer in a fixed match. As I coasted to the sandy shoulder, I hoped that Roderick hadn't got greedy and sold the jack and the spare off for beer money. Just before I pulled off, I caught a flash of white out the corner of my eye. I glanced back in the side mirror and saw a hottie in a white nightgown, complete with big, black eyes and long hair. By the time I got the parking brake on, she was gone. I'll never forget the look of absolute hopelessness on her face in that split second. I've since wondered if it was for her plight or mine.

After I had hopped out and headed to the back of the truck to dig out what I hoped was a decent spare, I heard the unmistakable grumble of a semi downshifting. At the crest of the small rise where I had taken out somebody's leftover party, the night was split by the arc of bright lights, and I gasped. For heading over the hill was a blood red, almost black, custom Peterbilt, running empty and wide-assed open. I mean, he must have been running about one-forty because the pipes were red-hot and sparks flew off the undercarriage as he scraped the asphalt on top of the hill.

However, my hopes of grabbing a ride and not wrecking a new pair of jeans went out the window as his lights started drifting my way. I knew the drunk sumbitch would never be able to stop, so I took off into the desert at a sprint, hoping any coyotes would have long since made for shelter. I got maybe twenty yards from the Suburban when the bastard plowed into it, spinning it around like a Jew kid's dreidel. Both back doors took flight, and the right side one damned near took my ear off, landing about five feet from me in a shower of water, mud, and safety glass. The crazy sumbitch took off like he had hit a bug. I don't think he slowed down and damned if I remember seeing any damage on the rig a-tall. I mean, I don't even recollect the lights even dimming. After a few seconds, the night returned to normal. The running lights of the trailer faded out purty damned quick, and I was back in the black of a desert night.

Cursing my lousy luck, I tried to figger a way back to something like civilization when I remembered the Nextel. I hoped that the impact hadn't flung it halfway to Phoenix. I crawled into the soaking driver's seat and felt around. I dug it out from under the passenger seat and, to my delight, it looked like it would work and still had battery left. As I keyed in the code Roderick gave me in case of emergency, hopped out, and began to pace the yellow line, I stole a peek at the dash-cam and damned if it wasn't humming along. I doubted the tape would show much but hoped that it might have caught a tag number on the big rig.

Naturally, Roderick didn't answer the damned thing. Some teeny bopper answered it between giggles. "Yeah?"

In my fury, I'm afraid I curled her hair and deafened her, too. "This is Hank. Tell your idiot fuck-buddy I'm stuck on the side of 491 near Naschitti and I need a damn tow. Some bubba-wit trucker damned near kilt me, and I've got a fuckin' flat to boot! Tell 'em to send me a ride, damnit!"

With that, I hung up and hoped Bobby would stop with the motorboat noises long enough to make the call. Then I set a new world record for the lug wrench toss, flinging the sumbitch about a mile into the night. Then, I heard a sound that had terrified me since grade school—the growl of a big, pissed off, and hungry dog.

I glanced over the destroyed rear of the Suburban and saw about a dozen yellow eyes headed my way at a slow lope. They were about a hundred yards from me and starting to spread out into a circle. I did some quick figgerin' and guessed that *if* Bobby had gotten the message, the truck should be here in about fifteen or twenty more minutes, assuming it was coming from Newcomb and not Shiprock or Gallup. If one of the other two, hell, it might be an hour.

I decided to go down to the rabies brigade fightin' and tried to remember if I had another weapon. I had silently slapped myself silly for chunking the lug wrench when I remembered the Big Bertha I had thrown the back after yah-yahing with some half-wit at the chain truck stop up in Shiprock over whether or not the carpet matched the drapes on the cute little blonde cashier and he offered to give me a free rectal exam with his work boot to back up his side of the debate. I was right, they didn't.

Sho 'nuff, the club was still back there and intact. The shaft was a bit... cock-eyed I reckon, but I hoped it would take a few mutts with it. As I emerged back onto the pavement, I noticed the growls had stopped and the eyes were arrayed around me in a semi-circle. They had crept up to within ten feet of me, and I noticed just how big the sumbitches were. They weren't as hefty as a Great Dane, and they weren't as streamlined as a Doberman, but they were still better'ern knee high on me, and I'm pushing six-foot-two and two-fifty.

Then, I heard something that I hadn't heard since college and damn sent me into either a flashback or hysterics. It was merely a deep bass *woof*, but the last time I heard that, I had been riding a motorcycle on a back road in South Carolina fleeing a hound dawg the size of a damn calf who kept pace with me despite me running close to eighty and the fact that he had to deal with a scrub pine-lined roadside. I knew right away that what I was playin' with wouldn't notice a golf club up the side of the head, being more Black Shuck than Benji.

I then decided to cool my jets out of the rain and watch only the back of the Suburban rather than twist my head off trying watch 'em all. Having made myself as secure as I could, given the circumstances, I hunkered down in the backseat and wished whichever idiot Bobby had called would come the hell on.

I was lighting a cig when I heard the ripping. Dumbass that I am, I checked to make sure that my pants were intact. Then, the big Suburban started to settle axle-deep in the sand on the right side. I giggled a bit and thought of that horrible movie about the Titanic from back in the day. But after making as sure I could without actually offering myself up as a snack, I returned to watching the gaping maw that was once the tailgate of the Suburban and stealing quick peeks over my shoulder to see if any headlights were en route.

I noticed that the dogs had made no move after about ten minutes and decided to see what was up. As I hopped off my rather absurd perch on the driver's side, I landed on top of the body of what I first thought was a buzzard, but soon recognized as a crow. I didn't see any obvious signs of it being a feast for the mutts, so I assumed it was just old roadkill. Then, I noticed that the dogs were gone, but that they *had* had a fuckin' field day on my right front tire. I mean, they ate the rubber, steel belts, and all. All that was left was the rim.

As I straightened up, I finally saw the swirl of the tow truck's lights appear over the rise. The guy just gave me a grin full of feathers as he hooked up the remnants of the Suburban. I flicked a cigarette butt in the general direction of the near-disaster and nodded at my ride. "Bobby Roderick's place after we stop at the nearest beer joint. I'll buy a round." He had no objection.

When I pulled up at Bobby's gate at four-thirty in the mornin', I unloaded the tape from the Super-8, grabbed my spare cigs, the unused Big Bertha, and whatever else I thought Bobby might want. Brandon, the driver, handed me the tow bill and simply said, with an accent that brought to mind either shamrocks or thistles, "Y'all be careful out there now. The Hunt will be on the prowl now. I'd stay off 491 for a few weeks." And then he pulled through the old rest area and headed back to Newcomb.

As I shouldered my load, I gave a low whistle of appreciation because Bobby had hooked me up again. A jet-black Ford F-150 hybrid sat in my usual spot, looking showroom-new. I knew better than to ask silly questions where it had come from, so I just headed into the office. I did notice with a shrug and a sigh that the F-150 had the same Super-8 setup the Suburban had.

Well, Ole Bobby was damn near giddy to see me and almost married me when he saw that I had saved the tape of last night's jocularity. After what seemed like a thousand questions, mostly about the semi that almost ended all this fun, Bobby decided to tell me what I already knew, but really didn't want to hear. Just before this, I decided to share with Bobby my plan to castrate the sumbitch in the red Peterbilt with a soup spoon if I caught up with him. I damned near thought Roderick was gonna swallow his beer bottle whole at that. He giggled like a virgin with a vibrator for about a minute before saying, "Youse won't see him again. I'd be more worried about what was coming next if it was me."

I twisted the top off another Bud Light, flicking the cap out the open door.

"Whadda mean, next? Last night wasn't good enuff? We had everything but damned Yul Brynner."

"Yeah, you had all kinds of fun last night. But what I'm interested in ain't showed yet. 'Sides, you still owe me four more nights, but after all the hassle, I'll up your rate to a grand a night, same stipulations as before. That should make ya happy."

"Yeah, that's peachy, but what the hell else is they? I mean, we had Nightgown Gal, Hellhounds, and what everybody seems to think was a Phantom Trucker. What else you want, Abe Lincoln?"

"It was the Mad Trucker, not no damn ghost. Now, the Sedan ain't showed and neither has the Hunt. Now, you mentioned something about stepping on a big old squashed crow the size of a doormat, didn't ya?"

"Yeah, at first glance I thought it was a buzzard, but after I really looked, it was just a crow. I remember seeing a few feathers in the grill of the Suburban as the guy put it on the truck, but damned if I remember seeing any fly or hearing a thud before the flat. Hell, I would've seen the big bastard dive bomb me head-on as smashed up as it was… that sumbitch wasn't a crow 'tall, was it? Just what the hell's goin' on?"

"Cool ya jets, speedy. What do youse know about the Navajo? Like their beliefs and stuff?"

"Not much, most of 'em are Christian. A handful still believe in witchcraft and all that other tribal hoodoo."

"Ya ever hear of a skinwalker?"

"Read Tony Hillerman's novel. That's about it. Barely remember it. I think it was a murder mystery."

Roderick gave me a blank stare for a second and then blinked. Bobby wasn't zactly an intellectual giant. After he let the horrible image of a book fade, he spoke. "Well, a skinwalker's basically a Navajo werewolf to simplify stuff. They can take all kinds of shapes—coyote, snake, crow. Lot of folks hereabouts think some of the old brujos can still either make ya one or are one."

"They change shapes… really. Lemme guess, if they stare at ya, they can steal ya soul, too."

"Well, yeah… hey now, I thought you didn't know nothing' 'bout 'em."

"Mmmm, as fascinatin' as all this is, I need forty or fifty winks, a shower, and a meal and maybe some sweet, young company. You still want me to go back out to 491 and play with the weirdness?"

"Sure do. Same old grind for the next few days."

"Okay, it's your money. I'll be back out there about eight. I'd try to get actual facts out of ya, but I'm sure the mumbo-jumbo would flow like shit inna sewer. I'm assuming the set-up with the camera's the same as before. I don't wanna know where it came from, as I'm guessing you 'borrowed' it. I'll bring the tapes back like always. Keep the Nextel handy in case the creepshow starts up again."

"What the hell happened to ole Curious George? The ghost genius? I figgered you'd die to hear about the Sedan and the Hunt, hum baby. Damn, the fun youse got coming next."

"I'd rather figger it out the hard way, like last night. Right now, I'm gonna shower and collapse."

"Suit yourself. See ya in the morning"

Well, I took the Ford back to my place and crashed like a jet that's out of gas. I slept for at least ten hours because I jumped up at six and had to haul ass to get to Gallup by eight. I did call my folks back in Carolina, more out of habit than apprehension. That night and the next went just fine. No wildlife, no big ole buzzards, no crazy-assed truckers. Just me, the desert, and the night sky. I had almost written off the weirdness of a few nights back when it all came back to me with interest on Friday. And I had such hopes for cashing out and things getting back to normal…

The whole mess actually started right before I quit on Thursday morning. Right at five, I was headed to Gallup to head back to Bobby's when I noticed a car. It was a big old black four-door sedan, like an old LTD or Impala from the seventies. Besides pushing forty years old, what made it stick was the fact that it followed me from Buffalo Springs almost all the way downtown in Gallup with its damned high beams on. I tried speeding up, slowing down, tapping the brakes—nothing helped. The idiot refused to dim 'em.

Right before I pulled over for gas and a fresh cuppa Joe or two, I noticed that the thing was damn near on fire. Steam was comin' outta the grill, from under the hood, and damned everywhere else. I figgered he had had the brights on while he followed me in hopes of find a gas station or a garage. But damned if he didn't just keep on truckin'. I saw the passenger side window come down, and an arm encased in blue denim shot out and pointed at me. He didn't give me the love finger, just pointed. I tried to remember if I had cut him off or anything, couldn't, shrugged, and did what I had to do.

Now, this next part really might make ya think I'm nuttier than a Planter's can, but I ain't, I promise. Everything I write about really happened, scout's honor. I hit Old 666 the last Friday bright-eyed and bushytailed, having spent the morning with the cute li'l blond cashier doing what comes natcheral, if ya dig me. Yup, she enjoyed it. Up 'til about two a.m., everything was routine. Right after the clock flipped and I headed out of Naschitti, everything went to hell.

It all started with what I thought was our old pal, Nightgown Girl. I was running about ninety when I saw a figure standing on the opposite shoulder. She was wearing a white dress, but it wasn't as flimsy as the other gal's. Oh, and she was tanner than the gal I saw before. Looked like a Mexican. The same wild hair was going on, and I swear she was cryin' and wringin' her hands and reaching out to me. Then I saw the bundle at her feet and realized who I was staring at. It was La LLorona, the Weeping Woman. There was what was left of a dry creek bed back down the highway about a quarter mile or so, and she must have been there looking for her children for more than a hunnerd years. Course, if she hadn't kilt 'em for a bit of strange, she wouldn't be here now. While I was distracted by her, the black sedan from a few days before returned, brights and all.

I damn near drove off into the desert and jumped a foot in the air, not the least because while I was ogling a dead chick by the side of the road, I had slowed down to a crawl. Only the pickup's acceleration saved me from being rear-ended. As I sped up to about eighty, the car kept pace, still smoking. I now saw it was a seventy-six, I'm guessing, Le Sabre. Big ole land-yacht. The black vinyl top had gone raggedy, and I saw spots of rust under the flapping pieces.

The guy driving must have been blind because he drove all hunched over the wheel like he was trying to see through a blizzard. He wasn't a beauty queen, either. His face was craggy; his hair looked like a bad bird nest built of gray twine, and he had a 'porn-stache' that was black as coal under a big ole hook nose.

As he crept ever more slowly up the ass of the F-150, the damn bottom fell out. I mean, rain, wind and lightning like a B-movie. I braved the elements long enuff to stick an arm out the window to wave him around. The damned rain put my just-lit Camel out. Naturally, this pissed me off. At damn near five bucks a pack, that's a quarter a piece.

The stupid sumbitch declined my offer and crept closer to the back bumper of the truck. Despite the fresh rain and runoff on the pavement, I gunned it. After about a minute, I noticed that the Le Sabre had passed me and was slowing down about a half mile ahead. The dumb bastard decided that real life was a movie and slung the big ole Buick across both lanes, causing me to invent about a dozen new curses as I stood with both feet on the brake pedal. After I had gotten stopped and made sure I hadn't crapped myself, I grabbed the golf club from the floorboard of the passenger seat and threw the door open.

"You crazy-assed mother fucker! I should ram this thing up your butt 'til I see brains on it! What the fuckety-fuck do you think this is? *Grand Theft Auto?* You could've fuckin' killt me!"

With a leisurely pull on his cigar, he nodded and grinned in appreciation. Now, one thing I will say for myself, I am a master of the dirty word. Just ask anybody who knows me… or either of my ex-wives.

"Oh, what I could do with that," he said. "Now lissen here, we ain't got time to be exchanging pleasantries. The rest of the fellas are gonna be along shortly. The Boss is rather pissed at ya, missin' work this long."

"What the *fuck* are you babbling about? I'm doing my job, and I ain't had a boss in close to three years. Any fellas you run with, I got no interest in. Now, move this ginormous piece of shit 'fore I knock it clean to Denver."

"That won't happen. Damn, boy, just cool ya jets. If I could still get to my 'toybox' back in 'T or C', I'd really show ya how to use that thing. But now, whatta mean, you ain't had a boss in years? Son, this is a steady gig if they ever was one, even if they ain't no money in it."

"First, you ain't my daddy, so quit callin' me son. Second, what the hell are you babbling about? Toyboxes in T or C? What the hell?"

"Damn, whatever ran you off wiped you cleaner than Granny's panties. You have no clue who I am or what I'm talkin' about or what *you* are?"

"I wouldn't know you if I woke up in bed with ya with yer name tattooed on my eyelids. I'm Hank Tolson, washed-out TV host, part-time delivery boy, and part-time used book pimp. And who the *fuck* might you be?"

"Son, they called me David Parker Ray when I was down here and able to romp. My toybox was where I'd take my… dates… for some fun. Ya know, whips, chains, saws, electric breast stretchers, the whole bit. I took out at least one a year. Then, after the sickness got me, I wound up in the Hunt, trying to work off what I'd done. When I could get loose, I'd freelance some in this ole hoss. And you, my friend, are needed. Play time is over." And the brave bastard took a step in my direction.

"You best back the galloping fuck up. I'll cave your skull in and suck out the juice. Now, if you are who you say you are, I'll be callin' the cops to pick ya up."

As I pressed the first digit of the emergency number, a blast of cold air roared down like wind shear and knocked it from my hands into the once-dry creek roaring beside the road. It *had been* just a ditch, but the rain and wind had turned it into a mini Grand Canyon.

As it tumbled to the bottom of the ditch, I saw the display flicker and then fade. Now, I knew I was fucked. Me and a crazy guy who thinks he's a dead serial rapist and mass murderer in the middle of nowhere in the rain. Great, just fuckin' great. Well, at this point, I decided that cowards are just brave men who live to fight another day, and I decided to head back to the truck and wait the loony out. I hoped that by the time his hands started to mildew, he'd just drive off. As I turned, the sumbitch grabbed my shoulder in a death grip.

"Now, now. You're not leaving yet, my man. The Boss and the rest of the boys are a-coming. In fact, I hear 'em now."

As he spoke, the wind picked up to at least thirty miles an hour. I mean, a steady gale. If it had been dry, sandstorms and dust devils would have been everywhere. The thunder and lightning, which had died down during our little chat, picked up. At least two big ole bolts hit within a mile from us, filling my nostrils with the stink of sulfur and possibly the stink of a well-done coyote too. I had decided to take idiot boy out and take my chances encased in about a ton of Detroit steel when, all of a sudden, about fifteen fellas on horseback popped out of nowhere and surrounded us. One of them had a monk's haircut and looked to be about seventy. He had a long white beard and wore a white robe trimmed with medieval-looking drawings of animals. He trotted forward, and I had to remember to close my mouth before I drowned.

"Ah, it seems we have found our missing venator in one piece. I was concerned that the... distractions would pose... difficulties in getting your attention. We have missed your skills in our Hunt for these last two-score years. I am getting older, and keeping these young brigands in line is a struggle. I require you to return to your penance."

"Whoa, whoa, whoa. What's this about penance? I never seen you before, and your problems fer sure ain't like mine. Sorry, but I can't help ya. You got the wrong man, fella."

As I spoke, I noticed that the surrounding horsemen had drawn closer. I could make out the shapes of hounds and heavily loaded game bags tossed over saddles. Some of them wore clothes that were at least two hundred years out of date, but a few wore stuff that I could have had in my closet. Of course, I couldn't make out a single face yet, but I blamed that on the infernal rain.

"No, sirrah, Ecce homo. The one I seek is the one I have found. Let us clear away these... toys and matters may become clearer."

With that statement and a funky hand gesture, the Le Sabre and the pickup disappeared. In their places stood two stallions, one a pale gray and one jet black. From the looks of 'em, either one could've won the Triple Crown walking. The fella who swore he was David Parker Ray mounted the black one with a sigh.

"Sure wish you'd been harder to find. I need all the time off my term I can get. Dying don't cut this here sentence short."

Like I had been slapped in the back of the head, everything fell into place. My interest in ghosts, my love of theatrics, and the joy I got from riding a fast car well, my nocturnal habits. I knew that the last forty-one years had been the merest detour from my destiny. I was a member of the Wild Hunt. Nay, not just a member, but a Master Hunter, charged with bringing the souls of the knowingly damned to bay before God. After six centuries, I had worked off the dregs of my sins and risen to second-in-command under St. Hubert. After another hundred years, my penance would be complete, and I would be allowed to finally enter Paradise. Having died a suicide, but secure in the True Faith, I was unfit for Hell, but in need of purification. Our Lord, in His wisdom, chose my penance to match my earthly role. As such, I rode with the worst of the worst. Men like Booth, Oswald, Gaskins, and Sutcliffe rode with us, doomed to a near-eternity without peace, bringing those who had followed their example to face the wrath of God. Only a few of those who rode with us had entered Heaven, Drake and Roland being two who came to mind. Now, I would resume my quest.

"Forgive me, Father, for I have sinned…" I began.

"All is forgiven, my son. Soon, very soon, you shall be with Our Lord. Now, let us away. Our quarry awaits."

Oh, if you were wondering, Bobby got his truck back. The tape showed everything up to David Ray getting out of the car, but he wasn't satisfied. As far as I know, Nightgown Girl, the Mad Trucker, and La LLorona all still prowl Route 491. No one noticed that I was missing for a few weeks, then my old lawyer flew out from LA and had me declared legally dead after a few months, and that was that.

Oh, and Hank ain't short for Henry. It was short for Herne.

TIME HEALS ALL WOUNDS?

Summer 1980, Caweetoolee Mill Hill, South Carolina

DORALEE GORDON WAS TWICE A WIDOW. ONCE TO THE CHEAP WHISKEY THAT kept the demons her husband, Warren, brought back from Germany at bay, and the final time to the cotton dust that finally filled his lungs in late 1979.

Despite her personal struggle, she birthed four babies and raised two to adulthood. The children, Kimberly and Warren Junior were both married to people Doralee didn't understand. Kimberly's husband, Ray Wilson, was a hippie. He wore his blond hair long and braided his scraggly beard and always smelled funny. She didn't understand the attraction, but Kimberly was happy, and Ray did support her so she could stay home and watch the stories with her momma every weekday.

The oldest, Warren Junior, was married to some Yankee bitch he met at college named Natasha, who insisted that her name be hyphenated to show how liberated she was. She was convinced that Doralee and the rest of the folks in Caweetoolee would turn her boy into some hideous redneck, killing small animals and hating Negroes and raping every gal he met. So she fought hard to keep Doralee's grandson, Donald, away, but Warren Junior insisted that the boy spend every summer helping Doralee in the garden and with the handful of chickens she kept, so he'd be self-sufficient like his granddaddy and daddy.

Warren Junior knew that growing up a city boy would mess Donald up and hoped that the lessons of the Hill would temper the hard edges a big city like Greenville would force him to have. Respect for elders, a working knowledge of nature, and an understanding of his roots would make the boy into a better man. So, that explains how a rambunctious ten-year-old came to be running through Doralee's living room at ten a.m. on a June Saturday.

"Bye, Grandma!" Donald shouted as he came darting through the kitchen, grabbing a banana and a chicken leg as he circled the big, round table. "I'm going to Levi's and to the crick and maybe to Missy's to swim!" the boy said in one breath, followed by, "Love you!"

"Slow down, Donny," Doralee said over her shoulder as she mixed cornbread for lunch. "You know they ain't no need to run in the house," she added, just before the crash.

As soon as she heard it, she knew it was bad. Even before the gasp of pain and tears started, she knew. As she entered the living room, she surveyed the wreckage. Her curio cabinet was intact on the outside, but the boy had busted the filigreed glass on one door and cut his knee pretty good, not to mention the knot he had raised below his bowl-cut bangs and the matching black eye. She gently yanked him up and guided him to the kitchen table. After filling a hot water bottle with ice and making him put it on his head, she grabbed a dishrag and cleaned up the cut and poured hydrogen peroxide on it, then sprayed it with some antibiotic spray, and put a big Band-Aid on it.

"I told you not to run in the house, didn't I?" she asked calmly, having dealt with this too many times to count in her sixty-two years.

"Yesum," Donald mumbled, trying very hard not to bawl and whine like he wanted. He knew that Grandma would just shush him, saying that boys don't cry about nuthin'.

"Is the cabinet busted up bad?" he asked, also knowing that his daddy would beat him silly if it was.

"The glass is broke, and I naturally ain't looked inside yet, but I think Mr. Robbins next door can cut me a piece to fix it," she said, pleased that the boy was worried about more than himself.

"I'm real sorry, Grandma. I didn't mean to. Honest!" the boy said, knowing that he was at fault *and* that if he didn't apologize, his daddy would be all kinds of upset when he saw him on July Fourth.

"I know, Donny. Now you go on and play, but be home by one. We're having pork chops for lunch."

"Yes, ma'am!" he said, and the boy was out the door and up the street before Doralee got to the wreckage. Aside from the door, the outside was fine, but then the old cedar cabinet had stood up to two moves and both Warrens' tempers over the years. Inside, most everything had survived in one piece except for her one memento of her one trip outside Caweetoolee by herself in the last forty years—a foot-tall ceramic Statue of Liberty she bought while waiting on Warren Senior to come home from Europe in 1946.

She remembered his letter word for word, especially that he would be coming into New York on April 30th on the *SS Carrier*. The statue and Warren

Junior were the only souvenirs she brought back from that trip. She gathered up the pieces and put them in a bowl and put it in the back of the cabinet behind some of Warren Junior's school stuff. She knew no one would notice because nobody paid the old cabinet any mind. In fact, she had heard Kimberly and Warren Junior arguing about whom would get it if she died at the hospital the last time her heart had acted up.

She decided then to call Mr. Fowler Hix, her lawyer, next week and change her will so that Donny got the cabinet and everything in it, just in case. She knew he'd appreciate it when he got grown. Then, Doralee went back into the kitchen to finish her cornbread and to cut up some tomatoes for lunch. The tears staining her cheeks vanished into the hem of her housecoat without another thought. With that, after Mr. Robbins cut her some glass and put it in, the old cabinet returned to its place in the background, the five fragments of the busted curio still in the chipped blue soup bowl, and the incident was forgotten. Hell, the incident was forgotten that day when Donny came home for lunch at full sprint, dragging the remains of his *Dukes of Hazzard* T-shirt behind him while he wept.

"Grandma! Missy broke up with me! She said I was a half-Yankee jerk, and when I argued with her and dunked her in the deep end of their pool, her brother, Jackie, beat me up when I got out!"

"Now, now, first, quit the bawling. She's just a girl, and there are a bunch more of them around. Second, Jackie's momma owes you a new shirt, and I'm gonna call her after we eat, if I don't just walk up there."

"Grandma, why are people mean?" Donny asked between stifled sobs and mouthfuls of cornbread.

"Son, that's just how the world is. All we can do is be better than most and hold on," she said, knowing that the two boys would be thick as thieves by morning and that the McCullen girl would be back to trying to steal a kiss from Donny after church by Sunday.

June 2008, Cheslea Falls, SC

DONALD GORDON WAS FED UP. HE WAS TIRED OF GETTING THE SHAFT AT his lovely job as Director of the Cheslea County Archives. His co-workers were twits, and the board that ran the place didn't know a city directory from a highway map but just loved giving him advice on how to store two-hundred-year-old diaries and century-old ball gowns anyway.

His apartment was a sty even by bachelor standards, so sitting around in his shorts while reading some crap novel and surfing the net for anything interesting was out. He did the natural thing. He got changed and went to the local dive, Captain Jack's. It was everything you wanted in a small-town watering hole, even if the nautical theme made no sense. There was old country on the jukebox, the bartender doubled as a bouncer, the waitresses were easier to seduce than whores in Vegas, and draft beer was a buck a mug until nine. By then, Don would be so wasted, he wouldn't care that the prices went up to five bucks. He'd either work hung over the next day or rely on the wonders of water, cheap cigars, aspirin, and coffee to get through, like he did most weekdays.

If he *did* decide to get laid, he knew that Susie, the flat-chested, but big-butted back-up bartender with thick blond curls would be happy to oblige as she had so many other times. Susie was really after a ring, or at least a round of shacking up, but she'd settle like everybody else.

Of course, Don didn't know it, but tonight would be a bit different. After about four beers inside an hour, Don noticed a guy standing near the stage, watching the house band try to tune up and harmonize. The guy was a classic ginger with dark red hair and beard and freckles the size of dimes all over his face and arms. Being five-eight, less than a buck-fifty, and paler than a ghost at high noon made him stand out even more, being surrounded by either farmer tans or the results of too many hours in the tanning bed. Don finally managed to focus through his beer goggles and was stunned.

"Bobby? Bobby Ricketts? Is that you, man?" Don hollered over the crescendo of general bar racket, mainly consisting of a broadcast of the Braves losing again, two dozen drunks discussing local gossip, and a band trying to remember how "Ring of Fire" went. The red head turned toward the noise and grinned from ear to ear.

"Donny? Donny Gordon? Damn, dude, it's been, what, fifteen years now? Twenty? How the hell are ya?" The redhead swept the bigger Donny into a bear hug. "I ain't seen you since we walked at App State. You and whozit, Nikki, still together?"

"Nope, darling Nikki dumped me about a month into grad school. Some professor decided to make her his project for the semester. Since all I was doing was working so we could live, and he had cash to waste and an office for quickies, that was it. What brings you to this pisshole anyway?"

"Don, old buddy, I am now an agent for one of LA's finest agencies. That band that has been assaulting your ears for the last three years is the next Hootie. I'm going to sign them to a record deal, as soon as the lead singer sobers up enough to speak English."

"Dude, Pappy Roberts *is* sober. He just sounds like that natural. So, you here for a while?"

"Nah, just long enough to do this and give out plane tickets to the band. Come out and see me sometime. We'll go hell raise somewhere classy. Here's the card. Call the cell since I'm on the road so much. See ya around, Donny."

"You too, Bobby. And I'll holler at ya when I'm out that way next. Call me next time you're over this way." Donald said this despite the fact that he had never been west of the Mississippi and probably would never cross it. He also knew that Bobby would never come anywhere near Cheslea. It was just one of those daily rituals Southerners are so good at.

The twinge in Donny's chest went as unnoticed as the click of the base reattaching to the skirt of the Statue of Liberty back in Donny's dark and empty apartment. The sudden urge to piss over came him as his old roomie headed back to the stage. You see, Donny had a bit of a heart condition that no one had ever caught, or so his mom had always said. Having an insurance deductible of a cool grand a year made routine physicals rare at best.

The next few weeks passed without any real incident. Don still worked every day, though he did finally get his apartment neat enough to bring Susie back a couple of times. She was such a sexual athlete, he never noticed the whispered "I Love You's" that came in the heat of afterglow. He sure the hell didn't say it back.

His mom came over once just after the Fourth of July, but since his dad's suicide five years ago, they just went to dinner and that was it. He only called her on her birthday and Mother's Day, but he did go see her up in Chambersburg every Christmas. Though he had to admit, it was more for the side trip to Gettysburg than the chance to get lectured about his failings as a son and to eat tofu and black bread.

Thanksgiving was spent at his Aunt Kim's house in Caweetoolee just across from Granny's. His mother had made it clear at Granny's funeral in 1989 that she'd only go back to that "bump in the road" in handcuffs. Don enjoyed seeing his cousins but was glad to be able to just give them back.

Just after Labor Day, he got an invitation to a regional history seminar in Atlanta that caught his eye. It was on the difficulty of finding employment records for textile mills after the parent companies had closed, which was right up his alley. The fact that the main speaker was Dr. Nicole Mauvine-Hitchens was gravy.

The rest of the summer passed like most of the last five years had—quietly. Don stayed close to home, saw Susie a bit more than he liked, and spent a week in Caweetoolee babysitting while his aunt Kim and uncle Ray went on a cruise. That cured whatever baby-craving he might have had. By the end of the week, he was ready to sell all four kids to the gypsies for a buck each.

Labor Day 2008, Atlanta, GA

The end of August, Don drove down to Atlanta and got checked into the Marriott and decided to go have a drink to get over the joys of driving in the center of hell. To his dismay, he found the hotel bar slap full of people, all of whom were there for the same conference he was. So he took off to Little Five Points to find a bit more relaxed spot to get his beer on. To his shock, the place was not crowded, but at a bar side table, he spotted darling Nikki herself, all alone and surveying quite a spread of empties.

"Hi, do you mind if I sit here? The place seems to be a bit full tonight," Don said, trying hard not to stare down her scoop-necked blouse.

"That's fin—holy hell, *Donny*! How are you, baby?" Nikki shouted as soon as she realized who he was. "How's the folks?"

"Dad passed away a few years back, but Mom is still Mom," he said with what he hoped was a charming grin, but was actually a leer. "How's the doc?"

"A bastard," she snarled. "Sonvabitch left me a month ago for some sweet little redhead with big tits."

Don chuckled at the irony, but held his tongue. It may have come late, but payback was still sweet.

"Well, I never thought he was real smart. But to trade down like that…" Don said. "You wanna talk about it?"

"Nope, just sit here and drink," the lady said. "Here, let's buy you a few. Four Wild Turkey shots here and…?"

"A double screwdriver and draft beer," Don said, turning back to soak in the sight of his ex in a state he'd hadn't seen in almost twenty years. The redhead still wore her hair in a ponytail, but now she favored sleeveless scoop neck blouses instead of long-sleeve peasant blouses. Unless he was mistaken, she still sunbathed nude, though, based on the lack of a tan line where her spaghetti strap had fallen off her shoulder. He was jerked out of his lustful reverie, just as he recalled her tan legs and love of going barefoot, when she spoke.

"So, you here for the seminar or do you live here now?" she asked, four more empties added to the six previous. He sipped his screwdriver, wincing at the crummy excuse for vodka they used. The next one he'd order a bit more specifically.

"Nah, I'm in South Carolina now, trying to run a small archives setup for the county. No pressure to publish and steady benefits. Where are you now? You still at Converse?"

"For now, but if the divorce goes through, I'm leaving at the end of the year. Winthrop wants me to run their women's history program. And I have no interest in seeing Dr. Dickhead around town."

"Huh, you'd be in my neighborhood. I'm in Cheslea Falls. Call me sometime, and I'll show you the sites."

"Donny, do you forgive me?" The question was whispered, but the look said volumes. Nikki wanted to be forgiven, or at least the whiskey did. "I know I shit on you back then, but I was young and selfish."

"Nikki, of course I do. No hard feelings. Now do you need another round?"

"No, I need… Don't make me beg, Donny. Just take me back and hold me and tell me everything will be all right, like you used to."

"Sure, just let me settle up our tab and we'll go. You at the Marriott?"

"I don't wanna go to my place. I wanna go with *you*, Donny."

"Okay, let me get us a cab."

It had been years since he had necked in a back seat, especially with an audience, but the attraction that he had buried for so long overwhelmed any concern about prying eyes. Besides, he was in Atlanta for a weekend. What were the odds of seeing said cabbie again, especially without a buzz on?

He was amazed at the way they fell into the old familiar rhythm. He knew exactly what to do and when and so did she, notwithstanding her condition. The fifteen-minute cab ride left them both in no real state to stroll through a hotel lobby, but the promise of further fun pressed them on.

Nikki did not respond to any of the attendees who sought her eye for even a second, so focused was she on her looming release. As soon as the elevator doors slid closed, she began to grope Don in earnest. Don broke their embrace only to press the nine button and to find his room key.

The blast of cool air on his exposed dick told him that Nikki was about to give him one of her hair-curling blow jobs. Just then the door chimed and slid open. Thankfully, the corridor was deserted. Nikki led him down the hall, using his semi-flaccid penis as a leash. As soon as he got the door open—on the third try—he and Nikki stripped each other to boxers and panties, respectively.

The two of them exchanged glances and then fell on to the queen bed, entwined in each other. Her gasps and his moans of pleasure filled the space where words do no good. Both knew, even through the alcohol, that there was no emotion involved, just pure need.

The only break came when Nikki asked Don to set the bedside clock radio for six a.m. as she kissed her way down his beer gut. As soon as she got all of him into her mouth, he reached down and, using that sign language only old lovers understand, got her to swing her body around and into the "69" position without disengaging.

Following a mutual orgasm and lengthy kiss, they moved into the missionary position. In an instant, both were twenty-one again, as attractive and instinctive as ever. The sex was athletic and intense. From missionary to cowgirl, to doggy and back to missionary, they rolled and contorted, crying out when release approached and sighing at its passing. After an hour, they both collapsed, as spent as tax refund checks on vacation.

"Damn," they both said at once with mutual grins and giggles.

"You were… beyond belief," Don said, trying to hide his pride in his performance.

"Well, Mr. Gordon, you did extremely well yourself." Nikki smiled back, the whiskey stench gone from her breath.

"Remind me why we quit doing this again," Don said, half-curious and half-asleep.

"Shhh," Nikki replied. "Just hold me and rest up. Tomorrow will be a busy day."

When Don awoke to the static-filled tones of NPR and rolled over, he was confronted with an empty room, unchanged from the previous evening save for his suitcase on the dresser and a pair of floral nylon panties at the foot of his bed. With a sigh, he slapped the off button on the clock radio and headed to the shower. As he passed the damp panties, he tossed them into the bathroom trash can with a sigh and got into a hot shower to get ready for a conference he now wished was over.

Unheard in an empty apartment some two hundred miles away, a soft click echoed inside a curio cabinet as the tablet bearing the date July 4, 1776, in Roman numerals slid back in place on a foot-high replica of the Statue of Liberty inside a chipped blue soup bowl.

The conference was. It just plain was. That was all. Don Gordon went through the motions and even got an invitation to speak at the one next year in Mobile. Dr. Nicole Mauvine-Hitchens did not speak to him the rest of the weekend, but she did give him a sad-eyed smile when he went to get a copy of her book signed. He gave her his card then, more out of habit than out of any expectation of a repeat performance or of seeing her again. He did not doubt her story of martial woe or that she had enjoyed their encounter as much as he had. But it was simply a fuck, not a round of love-making like it once had been.

The next six weeks ran together. More mindless days at work, whining about budget cuts, and missing out on a big donation of material by the VFW to Winthrop. More nights spent at Captain Jack's, drinking cheap beer and bedding Susie. Finally, he decided to burn a week of vacation up in Altamont, NC, before he lost it to the county's idiot leave day policy. The week he picked was the last week of October.

The week in the mountains did him some good. He hiked off about two inches of gut and breathed clean air. He hit some of the local hippie shops, but did not go home with any of the willing young things he encountered. Not out of any deep love for Susie, but mainly out a lack of interest and fear of finding thicker hair than his in intimate places.

For some reason, he was catnip to women either twenty years his senior or ten years younger. The ladies he was "supposed" to be dating weren't interested. He had long adjusted his sight accordingly, which was one reason he enjoyed sex with Susie so much. The age gap faded when she was such a willing pupil. Of course, the beer helped them both.

The only odd event that came close to bumming him out was a quick clip he saw on the late local news one night in his hotel room. Of course, it was the middle of the "crime and crash" report and he had tuned it out while he read a book on noted Altamont authors. Until he heard the name Kacie Saunders. He looked up with a start to see a cute brunette with a black eye discussing the mugger she had just fought off not three blocks from his hotel.

As he stared, gaping, it hit him that he knew her. It was Kacie! His prom date! The girl he left in Greenville to go to App State and major in history while she went to Furman. The last time he had seen her was high school graduation when she had given the valedictory address. She had aged very well, and he was pleased to see that she was still gorgeous. He was also glad to hear she was okay and that the guy had been caught minutes afterwards. After Kacie maced him and kicked in the nuts twice.

The tremor of pain down his back went unnoticed as he flipped the light off and headed to the nearest all-night diner for a late supper.

Far away, inside a blue bowl, a gentle click marked the reunion of the crownless head of Lady Liberty and the rest of her body.

The next couple of weeks passed as usual. No real drama. About a week before he headed up to Caweetoolee to see his aunt for Thanksgiving, a co-worker passed away suddenly. Well, as suddenly as a hypochondriac can.

Angela Dodge was renowned among county employees as having more aliments than anyone outside the Mutter Museum. She had back trouble, flat feet, headaches, constant nausea, eye issues, defective hearing aids in both ears, and a host of female aliments. Amazingly enough to Don, none of that killed her. She passed away from complications from Lasik eye surgery. Common consensus was she died from an infection she hadn't already taken seventeen antibiotics for.

However, the county closed down due to her forty-five years of service as a clerk in traffic court so that employees could attend her funeral in Columbia. With Don's luck, he got drafted as a pallbearer for the long time old maid, along with a few deputies and the county manager. The service was standard funeral home issue, but Don still teared up at Amazing Grace, even a bad copy from a copy on a hissing and popping cassette.

While walking back to his car, his natural grace kicked in, and he went ass over elbows as he tripped over a faded funeral home marker. As he cussed silently to himself and thanked the stars that no one had noticed, he glanced at the name on the marker and gasped. It was for a Tyler T. Philips. The only Tyler Philips he knew should still be alive and well in Greenville. Heck, Tyler was a three-sport all-star jock in high school and was a year younger than Don. Of course, a lot could change in almost twenty-odd years, but still, Tyler couldn't be dead.

He frantically searched his mental databanks for what *his* Tyler Philips' middle name was when it hit him. Tallmadge. After he dusted himself off, and wrote off the khakis he had worn, he whipped out his smartphone and ran a quick online search for the name before him and the date on the stone. Sure enough, the obituary popped up and everything matched. Tyler was killed at twenty-five by a drunk driver in downtown Charlotte while going to a concert.

As Don staggered to the car, he wrote the dull throb at the base of his skull off as some kind of weird reaction from the fall.

Meanwhile, back in Cheslea Falls, the Statue of Liberty regained her crown and knocked her home in the bowl onto its side. The upraised torch still lay on the rough wooden shelf, biding its time.

The Thanksgiving visit in Caweetoolee was bittersweet. He enjoyed seeing his aunt and uncle and the momentarily tame kids, but he felt a distance. While helping his uncle Ray chop some wood for the wood stove, Don decided to ask about it. Ray told him that he and Kim had considered divorcing due to long-standing issues now that the kids were old enough to handle it, but that he had just been diagnosed with prostate cancer. Ray reminded Don that he was always welcome, regardless of what happened.

"This is as much your home as mine, boy. You became the man you are across the road. No matter what your mama says, this is home. Always."

Don merely nodded, trying hard to imagine the upheavals that would result from either a divorce or his uncle's death. Neither prospect had a good outcome, so he shoved away.

"Hey, boy, I axed you a question. Have you heard from Missy lately?"

"What? Oh, Missy? Nah, not since Granny passed. Why? She famous now or something? What did she do, marry a serial killer?"

"Nope, she moved down your way. To Lake Catawba, I think."

Don nodded. Hundreds of folks lived on Lake Catawba. Hell, the damned thing had close to five hundred miles of shoreline and almost that many subdivisions. He had camped in the small state park on the shore on the Cheslea County side a few times and met with prospective donors at one of the big golf courses on the lake's northern shore, but he doubted he'd see Missy McCullen any time soon. Hell, he doubted he'd know her. After not seeing her for twenty years or hanging out with her since they both started junior high school, he probably couldn't pick her out of a lineup.

"Naw, she married some banker named Lancaster from Charleston. She comes home to see her daddy every Christmas and comes to ask about you almost every year," Ray said with a sideways glance at his nephew.

Ray felt that every man needed to be married at least once, and he knew that the Susie gal Don was currently fooling with wasn't wife material. He did hate that Don and Nikki had broken it off after college, but he knew better than to pick *that* scab again. Ray did know that Missy had told Kim that she had divorced the banker and bought the lake house to get out of Charlotte. Ray knew Don would go see his mom at Christmas, but he had hopes of getting the two together at New Years.

"Donny. Donny Gordon! Wake up before that wedge jumps in your lap, boy. Dang, I never thought you'd still pine for that girl. Let's get this done so I can get me a beer and another turkey sandwich before your aunt turns it into turkey casserole."

And that, Don thought, was the end of it. Missy lived on Lake Catawba, just like fifteen thousand other yuppies. He was stunned because he figured she'd wind up working at a gas station and pumping out a kid a year by a dozen different fellers. Good for her. Maybe if he got either real drunk or real, real horny, he'd give her a ring for old time's sake, assuming she was in the book and he could find her. But why the devil did he suddenly taste homemade sweet potato pie and cherry lip balm?

The next month was more hectic than most. Don drug himself to the mall once to get some stuff for the cousins and to the local five and dime to get stuff for his mom, aunt, and uncle. He did take Susie out to dinner at the new Italian place in town before they came back to his place. She stayed the night and left her toothbrush. Don knew it was on purpose, but didn't mind. Hell, it was almost Christmas. Let her think whatever made her happy.

The new girl at Captain Jack's, a leggy blonde with stripper boobs named Jasmine, had already caught his eye. She would be the New Year's present he *really* wanted to unwrap. What little there was he hadn't seen already, anyway.

The trip to Chambersburg was uneventful, though Gettysburg got bypassed this trip up. The joy of a Wednesday Christmas meant less time off. The good thing about that was less time to fight with Mom about when he would move closer.

The visit went really well. Mom even broke down and cooked steaks. They tasted like liver and were tougher than sun-dried leather, but she tried. She even mentioned coming to see Uncle Ray and Aunt Kim after hearing about Ray's cancer. It was the least stressful holiday visit he'd ever been on.

Thankfully, Cheslea County had a fairly enlightened policy on time off for New Year's. He got both the eve and the actual day off and burned a sick day to recover from both. He knew he'd be skipping the traditional black-eyed peas and collards since he hated both of them almost as much as he hated onions, but the booze would make up for it.

With that in mind, he headed up to the big liquor store at Boulder Mountain to load up for his New Year's party. He had invited some folks from work, some of the regulars from Captain Jack's, and both Jasmine and Susie. If the booze was really top-shelf, he might be able to pull off a threesome. Then, all hell broke loose.

As he tugged the crap-assed buggy with two sticky wheels down the rum aisle, he saw her. Missy McCullen. Looking better than a body had a right to. Her blond hair was still curly, and she had grown into her long and now quite shapely legs. From the looks of things, she'd had a kid or two, but got most of the weight off quick. The clothes, as befitted a yuppie, were designer. She had smaller boobs than he liked, but that was okay. He knew he was staring with his mouth open when she spoke.

"If you like it so much, why don't you… *Donny! Donny Gordon!*"

With that, she leapt over a display of fruit-flavored rum and damn near knocked him over.

"Hi, Missy. Long time no see," he said, glad he could still move a little even with the aches and pains of middle age. "What brings you here?" he said, playing dumb.

"Oh, got divorced and wanted to be on the water, but beach houses are so expensive. All that insurance. And the storms, mercy. How are you? You look great!"

Her enthusiasm had not faded from the time they'd been ten, he noticed with a grin.

"I'm fine. Still a bachelor. In fact, I'm hav—"

At that moment, in an empty apartment, in a dark and crowded wooden curio cabinet, Lady Liberty finally grasped her torch again after nearly thirty years. Once again, she stood whole and upright. Even the chipped soup bowl seemed to regain some lost luster by her presence.

With that, Don Gordon fell forward, dead. The verdict of the coroner after the autopsy was death by sudden heart failure, despite the fact that Mr. Gordon's heart was healthier than that of most ten-year-old boys. No other explanation made any sense. Mrs. Lancaster was treated for shock and released at the scene.

"One Man's Meat..."

IT ALL STARTED DURING A HALF-DRUNKEN CHAT AT A COCKTAIL PARTY IN Columbia. A small group was discussing their secret collections. It was odd enough to hear about the ex-NFL lineman with the collection of over five hundred Barbies and the preacher's wife who had beer steins from every city she'd ever visited ("and I drank every drop out of all of them") was unusual too, but he knew his would make their foreheads twitch.

"So, what's your kink?" the attractive graduate assistant from the history department he'd been eyeing all evening asked, the odor of scotch making his eyes blink like he'd just been hit with a laser. "And don't say ghosts! That's your day job."

"Actually, darlin', my day job at the moment is guest professor of folklore in the English department, but the ghosts have made that possible," he drawled. "I collect abandoned buildings," he said with a shrug.

"Abandoned buildings? Like old ramshackle barns and stuff?" the ex-lineman said too loudly, though in his defense, someone had chosen that moment to swap out CDs. "Where the hell do you put 'em?"

"I thought you lived in an apartment over near the old flour plant," the grad assistant whined.

"Oh no, I leave them where they are. I just take pictures and notes. And I do... we'll see it later if you like." He winked.

He hated trying to explain his obsession, especially to people he didn't know and had no interest in liking. Well, he had an interest in the grad assistant, but that would only last until morning. How did you explain the strange alchemy of Ambrose Bierce stories, WPA photographs, and a lifetime spent driving on southern back roads and the allure of the forbidden to the basically uninterested?

Contrary to popular assumption, the slim chance of discovering a new haunted site had nothing to do with it. He could indulge his boyhood fantasies of being a PI in a film noir or a dashing archeologist even in middle age. Plus, it was just the type of eccentricity one expected of a Southern bachelor of a certain age. At least he didn't ramble on about dead Confederates or paint his house in team colors.

Thankfully, he was spared the effort when the conversation turned to the latest political gossip, involving a state senator known for his race-baiting, his underage black boyfriend, and naked water balloon fights in the State House. Of course, alcohol was to blame. Most of the crowd expressed disappointment but still gave him a strong chance of being Governor in two years since he was a Republican in South Carolina. That tale prompted a long chat about great political scandals, which he escaped from only after the graduate assistant mouthed several obscene ideas in his direction. That was the impetus that got him to head toward the door, followed by her after a discreet interval.

The next morning, he awoke to a dull ache in his back, a mouth full of raw cotton, and pain above his right eye like he had been stabbed. To his bemusement, she was still there, cocooned in his comforter in the fetal position until only her face was visible. He grinned at the faint memory of the night before and the wonders he hath wrought. Then, he rolled out of bed, did his usual morning rituals, found some dirty jeans and a clean turtleneck and headed to the kitchen to fix breakfast, hoping his conquest was not a rampaging vegan or PETA true believer, as he had a serious Jones for bacon and eggs. And coffee, for God's sake—coffee and aspirin.

It was pleasant, as far as post-coital feeds go. She liked his coffee, ate as much bacon as he did, and even washed the dishes afterwards. Hell, she didn't even change the TV from the all news channel. She had showered and put back on her blouse and skirt from the night before. They made quite a couple—him sprawled on the couch reading the news crawl and her scanning the rows of book spines that lined the walls of the small living room with her bare feet up, but demurely crossed at the ankles, on the third or fourth-hand battered coffee table. A cozy domestic scene, even if he wished she'd leave so he could recover from the exertions of the previous evening.

But then, she had to ask.

"So, I'm dying to know more about this abandoned building deal. Is it just empty houses, old factories, or what? Why those? Why not historic places or battlefields or even graveyards?"

"Are you really interested? Because it's really quite dull. And you don't need to impress me. I already said I'd call you for lunch this week. But if you're really interested, I'll try to explain it. Hell, it might be easier to go find one close and let you see for yourself."

"Men… always thinking all us women want is a commitment or plain out monkey sex. Obviously, I'm interested since I brought it up. I'm still casting about for a dissertation topic since the lives of first wives of South Carolina Governors since statehood is about as interesting as watching ants fuck, and I already plowed the field of Female South Carolina pols who did what first for the ole MA. I was actually thinking about doing something up your alley even before last night's… carnival of sin."

"Like what? Why a grown man plays ghost hunter? I thought folks saved psychobiography for dead poets and serial killers, not boring old folklorists. I'm flattered, but honestly, I'm barely worth a high school essay. Not a career maker like a PhD dissertation."

"It wouldn't be just you. Other folks have done books of ghost stories before. Men and their fragile egos… I was thinking about going back to the WPA folks and coming up to today. Motivations, training, influences… all that stuff. Try to paint a picture of a ghost story expert through time. Why did writing in dialect stop? Why are the same stories recycled over and over? I think it might be interesting, and I'm the one I have to amuse with the research. So, why abandoned buildings?"

"Well, let me ask you a question or two to answer yours. You ever read any Ambrose Bierce besides *Owl Creek Bridge*? Especially *The Middle Toe of the Right Foot*? If not, read that story. It will help explain some of it. So, where exactly are you from? I know you're a Southerner by your accent. You from South Carolina?"

"I've read some Bierce, but mainly the Civil War stuff for an undergraduate class. I'll look it up. I'm sure it's on Google books," she said, inwardly smiling at the faint grimace of disgust he made at the mention of books online. "As far as where I'm from, I'm from South Carolina all right. Down near Marion, as a matter of fact."

"Okay, then you can see what I'm talking about. You're driving down a stretch of two-lane blacktop when you catch a glimpse of a house surrounded to the doorstep with scrub pines. Or standing out like a sore thumb on the same lot after the loggers have gotten everything else off. Now picture that same house forty, fifty years ago surrounded by cotton…hell, or tobacco…or maybe even corn, from horizon to horizon. Wouldn't your curiosity be piqued by who used to live there…what they did for fun…why they left?"

"Yeah, I can see the picture, but we already know the story. C'mon, how many books of oral histories about sharecroppers and tenant farmers have been done? Hell, I think I wrote a paper on the literature as an undergrad. I really don't need to wonder."

"Okay, what if the house was there first? What about the hand-hewn barns that are now just rattlesnake condos? The schools and warehouses left for the elements? People tell their stories with more than just words, right? And that's the attraction of all of it—the houses, the ghosts..." He trailed off, becoming frustrated by his inability to convince her.

"I suppose, but I still don't see it. Sorry, I guess I'm not the romantic you are. Not that there's anything wrong with that. It's actually kind of sweet."

"Well, I suppose the only solution is to put boots on the ground. If you want to understand the attraction and get some of these juicy stories, c'mon."

"Um, okay, you don't strike me as the axe murderer type, so lead on, Macduff. Where to?"

"Little bump in the road out past Congaree Park. It's covered up with abandoned stuff, like a buffet."

"I'm assuming you're driving? And can I ask a favor?" she said, making a sweeping motion down her torso.

"Yup, and of course I'll run you by your place so you can change. I'd recommend some hi-tops if you have any. And some already beat-up jeans."

"Okay, let me grab my purse. And, oh, Great White Hunter, you might need some shoes yourself..." She laughed as she headed down the stairs.

"Oh? Yeah..." he mumbled as he grabbed a pair of beat-up hiking boots from under the coffee table.

The drive from his river-view apartment in a converted warehouse to hers in an old, converted Victorian pile on Senate Street was pretty quick. Since it was a sunny Saturday in January, traffic was a lot lighter than it had been a few months before during football season. And wonder of wonders, for once he caught all the lights.

As they rode, she regaled him with her adventures in academia, from high school salutatorian—yes, she held a grudge—to her present position as graduate assistant and doctoral candidate in search of a topic. He noticed that she glossed over the previous night, showing no sign whether it was the rule or that he was an exceptionally lucky exception. He listened with all the clucks and grunts of someone engaged by the topic at hand, but his mind was elsewhere, as he soon proved by missing the turn to her place, despite her repeated reminders.

"Senior moment." He grinned, hoping that charm would mask his wandering mind. To his relief, it worked. He maneuvered the car through the myriad of one-way streets and found a spot in front of her place.

"I'll be right back, now. Don't you leave me," she said with a wink and then dashed through the front door.

After only about ten minutes, she re-emerged, wearing a man's flannel work shirt, jeans that were just tight enough, and some duck boots. The image brought to mind a model en route to a sporting goods shoot, among other less pure thoughts.

"Okay, done is done" she said, sliding across the seat to give him a quick peck on the cheek before nearly instantly returning to her spot and buckling her seatbelt.

"Wow... Good heaven, Ms. Harley, you're beautiful," he said, doubting she would catch the reference to a thirty-year-old hit wonder. The rapid spread of pink across her cheeks told him that she didn't catch it, but enjoyed the compliment.

"Okay, now, where to? Aren't we wasting daylight?" she asked as he pulled out.

"Like I said, a spot near Congaree National Park. It's only about fifteen minutes out, so we'll be able to hit several spots and still be back in town in plenty of time for me to buy you that dinner I promised."

"Sounds good. I'm already hungry."

So they headed out toward the empty hulk of Williams-Brice Stadium, which would have been filled to capacity just a few months earlier, and the State Fairgrounds, now bare and deserted as well, and drove through the industrial pockets that stretched toward Interstate 77, connecting the city to the rest of the world. In a few minutes, they went under the interchange, and the road narrowed to two lanes from the four it had been, and he spoke for the first time in a while.

"You ever read any of my books?" he asked.

"Yeah, the first one, about the haunted graveyards. Haven't read any of the other ones. School tends to kill my leisure reading. Why?"

"Well, there's a ghost story about this road we're on. Bluff Road. Wanna hear it?"

"Yeah, I guess," she said warily.

She wasn't a huge fan of ghosts and certainly didn't want to meet one. She had had mild misgivings about this jaunt from the start, but his seeming normalcy had tamped that down. Well, that and his surprising continued interest in her. None of her other conquests had shown any interest in her the morning after. Part of that may have had more to do with the imminent arrival of wives to town or dozens of other reasons, but he had been the exception. Now, she was out of her comfort zone and off her turf. She tried to rally memories from self-defense classes past and cursed herself for coming out to the sticks with this... stranger. Despite her small-town roots, she was a city girl through and through. *But let's get this over with and get back to town. Then we'll play the rest by ear*, she thought.

"Hello, anybody home?" he asked. "You're a bit younger for the senior moment excuse. So, you wanna hear it? I promise it's pretty tame. No blood and guts at all."

"Sure. And, sorry about that. Riding always makes me zone out. That's one reason I avoid the bus," she said with a weak grin.

"Okay, now let me see if I can remember it. Oh yeah, back in the forties, a young nursing student was coming home from Charleston to see her deathly ill father. It was a crummy night. Rainy, ground fog everywhere, standing water everywhere. The deer were probably stirred up, too, since this would have been the boondocks back then. Heck, I'm betting she was probably the only car on the road when it happened."

"What happened?" she gasped, then flinched as she knew she had broken one of the rules of being a good listener.

"Well." He grinned. "Further down, this road runs into Highway 601 just above the Congaree River Bridge. And there is where our story truly begins. One way or the other—my guess is a deer darted across in front of her—our nurse-to-be managed to hit the edge of the bridge head on. She was thrown from the car through the windshield into the river below."

"So much for no blood and guts," she muttered to herself.

He continued without even acknowledging her interruption. "Took folks a couple of days to find her body because the river was up with all the rain. The story has it that she didn't have a scratch on her. Since then people have reported seeing a young lady in a dirty, white, old-fashioned nurse's outfit, complete with cap, walking along the roadside both along 601 and Bluff Road. She normally appears during severe thunderstorms and late at night. If you stop and give her a lift, she asks to be taken to an address on Senate Street to visit her dying father. After you get to about where the road widens, *poof!* She's gone. All you have to show for your kindness is a wet seat full of muddy leaves and pine needles. I've heard that if you drove on to her destination, her mother or brother would give the straight dope. I've also heard that the house is long gone now, too. So no need to fear any nocturnal uninvited guests." He grinned.

"She...doesn't actually get home, does she?" she asked with more fear in her voice than she realized.

"Nah, like I said, just out here in the sticks. A-ha! Our first stop," he said, coming to a stop at a lot completely covered in pines except for the gray bulk of a house barely visible from the roadside. "This is one I think you'll dig. It's kind of like visiting Granny."

With that, he found what could only be called a track through the edge of the pines, which was bordered by brambles and carpeted with wisteria runners from the neighboring lot. She followed, wishing she had grabbed a baseball cap to keep lord knew what out of her hair. The soggy ground squelched and gurgled under their feet until they arrived at the front door of the house.

It was a classic shotgun house, complete with the central hallway. Every pane of glass had long since been broken by the unerring aim of local daredevils and their varied missiles. As they approached, he made sure that no new locks had appeared and tried to open the door. Due to the humid summers and soggy winters, the door and frame had both swollen and shrunk so many times that they were almost one. She was about to suggest trying the back door when she recoiled at the shrieking crash of the door being kicked in and at the flying splinters.

"The hell? Damnit, now we'll have cops from three counties all over us!" she said, shaking chunks of wood from her hair. "I thought you said this was all legal. I don't remember signing up for breaking and entering."

"Relax, just had to use my master key. The back door is probably as stuck as the front was. Besides, now I'll have an excuse to ask for a massage later. As far as cops coming, I doubt the neighbors heard it."

"Well, I just hope it was a one-time thing, Mister Macho. Otherwise, our first stop may be our last."

They stood in the hallway for a second and got their bearings. The front rooms were a living room on the left and a bedroom on the right. The two doors a few feet away, she guessed, would be the kitchen and another bedroom.

"Wow. All the furniture is still here. And the clutter," she said, kicking a stack of old, yellowed newspapers over as she entered the living room. "I guess they had to leave in a hurry."

"Maybe. From the looks of things, I'm guessing some kind of resettlement. Farm Security maybe? I'm willing to bet if we kept walking toward the back of the lot, we'd find a helluva a gully. Say, that pile of papers you just relocated, any dates on those?"

"Let's see… yeah, I think so," she said, wiping the grime away from the masthead. "Looks like some kind of agricultural bulletin… from the fifties. I can't make out much more than that right now."

"Yeah, that makes sense. Erosion probably killed the profitability of the cotton farm, and these folks got relocated into Columbia on our dime. Check out the pattern on that couch. It's blinding even through the dust."

"Well, yeah, but I've got a buddy who'd kill to have that hand-made hardback cane seat chair in the corner. Thing's probably worth a grand to the right person. Say, you know what I *don't* see? A radio cabinet and a phone."

"The radio probably went to town if they even had one. I doubt they even had a phone. If they did, out here it would have been on a party line, and I'm guessing Ma Bell grabbed it back. Let's see if the bedroom holds any treasures."

The bedroom looked better from the hall. The ceiling had collapsed next to the light fixture sending plaster, asbestos insulation, and all matter of leaves, feathers, and eternal onto the bed below. Add some water and the mattress had no chance. All that was left was what looked like a queen-size metal bed frame with a large pile of rubbish and steel straps and springs under it.

He braved the bouncy floorboards, which offered up the prospect of gangrene or worse, and his fear of whatever four-legged critter might now be living in the room to try a drawer on the dresser across from the bed. However, time, water, mold, and rust had conspired to seal them all shut tighter than Fort Knox during a bank run. He decided the closet was not going to offer much more success.

"Well, let's check out the kitchen. I'm wondering what's in the pantry," he said.

"Why? Getting hungry?" she laughed. Her initial fear had faded into a driving curiosity.

"Nah, not yet. But later, maybe," he said with a pronounced licking of his lips that drew the desired giggle.

The kitchen was still in decent shape. The wood stove stood under its flue, which was now lying atop the cooking surface. The pantry was bare to the wooden shelves, except for a few mouse carcasses. The sink was empty, but lacked any hardware, which led them both to believe that the inhabitants had lacked running water but got by with a well and outhouse. The outhouse speculation was confirmed by the lack of any indoor plumbing. The only thing of interest in the kitchen was a full set of orange Fiestaware, which elicited a squeak of delight from her, followed by a firm headshake from him. The remaining room, what must have been the children's room, was a complete bust. Some sheets of peeling blue paint and a bare, beaten-up floor was all they found. With a shrug, he motioned her to take the lead, and they returned to the waiting car.

"Well, you hooked yet?" he asked hopefully.

"Getting there," she answered. "What's next?"

"Well, I thought we'd check out a Rosenwald school down the road a ways and then we'd see how late it is."

"A Rosenwald school? What's that?"

"Gee, I'm playing teacher already. Guess it'll be good practice for when the kids come back from break. Julius Rosenwald was president of Sears back in the early part of the twentieth century. He got involved with Booker T. Washington and decided to help with black education in the Jim Crow South. He put up the money for, like, five thousand schools if the community would either raise some matching money or donate some labor. Basically, until after World War II, it *was* the rural black part of separate but equal education."

"Okay, gotcha. Now, no more breaking and entering. You're too cute for jail, and I'm too young."

After about a half-mile, they pulled into a muddy driveway that was once paved with gravel and parked next to a rather unimpressive-looking, white clapboard building that sat atop piles of river rocks.

"Gee, are you sure it's safe to go inside? She's not looking very stable on those rocks."

"Trust me. Those rocks have held this building up under even more weight than my fat self. Somehow, I doubt your extra few ounces will hurt much," he said, grabbing his midsection with both hands.

"Yeah, you're so *huge*," she said back with an eye roll and gentle shove in the arm. "Besides, I'm not a big fan of sculpted, pretty boys, remember?"

With that bit of banter, they walked to the rear of the building and entered. There were two large rooms, each flanking the center hall. Both rooms were empty, but the gouges and scrape marks on the heartwood pine floor showed that both rooms had been heavily used.

"Got this place put on the National Register," he said, his pride evident in the statement. "It's the only Rosenwald School in the county in the original spot. I swear, some days, you can sit in this hall and actually hear the slap of bare feet on the floor and droning of the teacher on either side. Hell, the way things look now, this ole barn will probably be whatever legacy I leave that's worth leaving, even with the books."

"It's nice. Wonder why no one uses it anymore?"

"Well, no indoor plumbing, for one thing. It's out here in the middle of nowhere. And after the big spate of school consolidation after desegregation, I bet the school district forgot about it. Heck, have you ever noticed the number of vacant schools in this state? I don't mean the ones that somebody has leased for a buck a year or something, but all these community schools just sitting empty. Ain't anything but a damned disgrace… Anyway, we didn't come out this way for you to listen to me whine about all that. Let's see what time it is… crap… we need to start back."

"Why? It's just four-thirty."

And then, the rain came. Unnoticed by our intrepid urban explorers, the puffy clouds in the blue sky they had left under had been replaced by a thick blanket of gray, low-hanging clouds that had just decided to dump their cargoes over southern Richland County.

"Um, well, that's one good reason," he laughed, and then he saw the momentary wave of panic sweep over her face. "I honestly doubt Swamp Girl will show up. Hell, all she is is a fancied-up urban legend. Don't worry about it. Heck, the way it sounds, I'd be more worried we don't sink to our waists going to the car."

With that, they took off at a sprint to the waiting car, mud flying up like the wings of Hermes. Despite their speed, they were both soaked to the skin and had coated their jeans in mud from the knees down.

"I am so sorry. When we get back to town, I'll toss this stuff in the wash while we go eat," he said, knowing and hoping that waiting for them to dry would present opportunities for more nocturnal fun.

"That's fine. I just need to go back by my place, shower *again*, and change. I'm guessing we're done?" she asked as they backed back onto the pavement.

"Yup. If you're ever gonna understand it, this should have done it. If not, well, I dunno what else to try. No reason to get double-secret pneumonia to beat a dead horse. So, any preference for supper? I certainly hope we still have a date."

"Of course we do. You don't think I wrecked a good pair of jeans for a one-night stand, do you? As far as food goes, a lot of it. I need to keep my strength up, ya know." She winked.

"Hmmm… well, I know you eat meat, thankfully… How does… What the hell is this idiot doing?"

"What?"

Behind them, but gaining fast through the rising ground fog and shade-speckled dusk, was an old-fashioned horse and carriage. They both could see the driver maniacally whipping the two horses, both of whom had shed their blinkers and were coated in foam. She turned her wide-eyed gaze from the fogged back windshield to his profile.

In answer to her unspoken query, he said, "I have no idea what the devil that is. I'm guessing it's a ghost, but I've never heard the folklore behind it. No real pair of horses is able to move at that pace, especially since I'm now doing sixty. Sorry, love, but I'm as in the dark as you are. Hopefully, when we hit the four lane in a few, the lights and extra activity will make it return to its shadowy origin."

"Damnit, somehow I knew. I knew this would happen. It was all going too well. This is why I should have just done the damned walk of shame this morning."

"Honey, you can't think I planned this little encounter. Hell, Swamp Girl is just an urban legend with a rural setting. I'm sorry for the upset, but in just a second we'll be back in town and laughing it off."

Sadly, he had no idea how wrong he was. At that moment, the car reached the center of a small bridge, barely more than a culvert with a guardrail over a small stagnant branch. As soon as the tires hit dead center, the car stalled out. He grabbed the steering wheel with his left hand, locked his elbow, and threw his right arm across her chest.

As soon as the car stalled, she let loose with a wail otherwise only heard in Hell. The carriage and its horses swept past on her side of the car and, despite the lack of clearance, made it by without leaving a mark on the car. As it passed, the staring, yet unseeing eyes of the horses showed no signs of life. The skeletal driver grinned through the greenish pallor of his worm-ravaged face, showing an alarming intelligence about his situation. A lace-cuffed arm emerged from the coach and shook a bony fist at the dumbstruck couple, the faint glow off the mist illuminating plainly the FH in script on the signet ring it wore. The lid of the chest strapped to the rumble seat flopped noiselessly, its cargo having long since moldered away.

As soon as all of it cleared the far end of the bridge, the horses reared in unison and bolted into the swamp, dragging coach and riders along without regard for any obstacle. After mere seconds, the horrible image faded away, leaving the gurgle of the branch and the black bulks of trees just outside the arc of the car's headlights.

They both sat there in stunned silence for a few seconds. Then, the appearance of headlights behind them brought them back to reality. He quickly restarted the car, and they drove back to Columbia in silence. He stopped off at her place and told her he'd call in the morning to see about a rain check on dinner. She simply shook her head and asked if she could go with him. He nodded yes and off they went.

The two of them returned to his apartment and ordered Chinese takeout. As they ate and listened to the stereo and waited for the washer to finish, the unreality of their encounter faded, eclipsed by scholarly curiosity.

"Well, I think some research is in order. Where did it come from? Who is FH? What happened to the car? Why did it wreck?" The questions came out in a torrent. "If you have a spare laptop, I'll see what we can find."

"Huh?" he said, having spent the last minute or two appreciating how good she looked in an old pair of sweats and a very threadbare T-shirt, even an oversized one. "Yeah, I'll grab it in a second. I dunno how much we'll find tonight, but it's worth a shot."

He got up and walked to his desk. He grabbed his laptop from its spot in his messenger bag and cut on his computer, flexing his left arm all the while.

"Damn that hurts," he muttered, hoping she wouldn't think it was age as he crossed back to the couch and handed her the laptop.

"I'll give you a rubdown later. That should help spur you along." She winked. "That was very sweet of you in the car to try to protect me. I do declare I owe you one."

"Then we better get to work and see what we can find before the clothes get done."

The next few hours were filled with the clicking of keys and grunts of discovery. The sum total of their labors seemed sparse, but explained those few seconds of sheer terror on the bridge.

FH was Franklin Herries, a Congressman from South Carolina in the 1790s and a major land speculator and swindler in the middle part of the state. His favorite marks were his fellow militia veterans who received land grants as bounties in lieu of cash for services rendered to the cause. Hopkins would buy these grants for pennies on the dollar and then sell parcels to the state and national government for astronomical sums. In about 1825, Herries sued a neighbor of his son's over the maintenance of a bridge over Gum Tree Branch of Congaree Swamp. The jury was packed with Herries's debtors and hangers-on, and he won his case. Of course, the damages awarded were stratospheric for the minor injury caused—a slave of Hopkins's had lost a toe to a snapping turtle while the bridge was under repair—leaving the loser with one of two options: sell out to Herries or bankruptcy.

The neighbor's young daughter, knowing the stakes, decided that if Herries had a minor scare, he might leave her father in peace. The young lady decided to play a prank on the Congressman, but it would have tragic results. She climbed a tree near the bridge in question and waited for the rumble of his coach down the dirt road. She knew he would be on the road because his former commander in the militia hosted an annual party to celebrate his troops' victory over a handful of British regulars every January twentieth.

Herries came through at his expected time and, just before his carriage reached the approach to the bridge, the girl leapt from her perch to the road below. As she hit the ground, the rest of the story was clear from their earlier experience. The frightened team stopped and reared, then bolted into the swamp. The fist shaking came as Herries recognized the guilty party. The coach was never found, and the driver was thought to have killed Herries and robbed his body.

Of course, no good deed goes unpunished, and the girl's plan failed. Hopkins's son, James Wilkinson Herries, demanded full and immediate payment of the damages to pay for his father's monument at the State Capitol in Columbia. The girl's father shot himself, and she moved to Alabama and married a planter named King. Afterwards, she faded from history.

Creek Walking

A MILL HILL WAS JUST ABOUT THE PERFECT PLACE TO GROW UP, ESPECIALLY back in the eighties when the mills were still running. If you were a boy from ten to about fourteen with a tendency toward being a bookworm and a loner, it was dang near paradise. If you got a wild hair and decided to get up a ball game of say, roll-the-bat, or tackle football, or any other kind of minor mischief, there were enough kids around to make it possible. But you didn't have a crowd of folks underfoot all the time either.

As a kid with a budding fascination with maps and books of all kinds, the infrastructure that surrounded me was enough to leave me gasping like a lush in a brewery. I had two mainline railroad tracks and a half-dozen spur lines that exercised a magnetic, though illicit, attraction. The spur lines made for excellent shortcuts, if you didn't ride a ten-speed yet and didn't care if the rent-a-cops from the mill gate yelled at you. However, the combination of ill-kept crossties and gravel was hell on the rims of anything less stout than a BMX special, and no kid was dumb enough to risk their main transportation to a known hazard.

Now, the unknown ones... If a train was coming, it was going slow enough that anybody could dodge it, unless you were asleep or dead. Ah, but the main lines, now those were the meat in my sandwich. Their attractions included three trestles to romp on, two of which crossed the river, one a good hundred feet high and the other a mere twenty or so. The third merely crossed a two-lane highway about ten feet high. It served as a clubhouse and launching spot for various expeditions. The lower trestle was the main thoroughfare between the two towns. We would cross it at all hours to see friends, goof off, fish and generally treated it as a footbridge. When the occasional train showed up, we would reluctantly move to one side like vultures forced to leave road kill. It also served as practice for the top trestle.

Despite both of them being about the same length, the top trestle was the real deal. The seventy-five or eighty-foot height difference was why. Well, that and the fact that the bottom one had sides and it didn't may have played a role, too. The top trestle was approached by two sides of an "S" curve that left you blind to an oncoming train. Practice had taught us that you had about thirty seconds to reach one of the concrete pillars, jump the four feet to the top of it, and hunker down under the rails or see if you could fly yet. A locomotive whistle at close range focuses the mind as well as combat, in my opinion. None of us tried to fly, but there were a few times that it seemed like the best option.

For the older kids, timed trips across the top were as good as playing chicken to test one's budding manhood. We couldn't do the usual side-by-side racing because it just wasn't wide enough, and no one wanted to take the heat if an unadvised jostle left one of our buddies a smear on either the riverbanks or tracks below. Hell, none of us could begin to try to imagine how we'd explain it to the poor soul's parents.

Now, your first exposure to the top trestle would leave you terrified. Many a soul would get no more than ten feet out, look down and become paralyzed, sprinting back only after hearing the gales of laughter and the finest crude insults a preteen mind can muster. On average, it took three tries to cross it, and most first-timers had to step on every single crosstie. After a few trips, you could skip ties and otherwise show off.

Considering my dad worked for the railroad that owned the trestle, I made sure I was well hidden before any trains came, not knowing when one would stop and have us all arrested for trespassing.

However, the network of highways and roads offered little appeal for those of us who couldn't drive yet. They mainly served as obstacles, looming as large in our minds as the Alps in winter or the Sahara at high summer. But the back alleys, those magical gravel goat paths, those were the bomb. In spots, you caught them after they had been paved with either concrete or asphalt, and those served as impromptu drag strips and Olympic tryouts. Of course, after about two or three years of crummy drainage, the asphalt would fail and the potholes would rival small ponds and be a bigger risk to a bike than a pissed-off pooch coming at a full run.

They ran all over town, mirroring the streets. They mainly served as routes for the trash truck and were meant to offer access to the garages behind the houses, but us kids used them as junior interstates. Besides, everybody parked on the street just about, and you played in the road and rode on the back alley. That's just how it was.

The back alleys offered some means of escape if you needed it and a place to indulge any vices you might have, especially smoking. They were less likely to be watched by every set of eyes that was home, since everybody in town knew who every school-aged kid belonged to and had no issue with reporting any mischief in gory detail. The fact that some lots ended rather abruptly at the back alley's edge gave some of us a chance to show off our cliff-climbing skills for an appreciative audience of our jealous peers. Not to mention that the back alleys gave us access to the garages.

What treasures they held. They had originally been built to hold Model As and their related pieces and parts and had been given over to storing the accumulated crap that you gather after fifty years at the same address. Lucky indeed was the kid who had a key to one of these storehouses of dreams. It was, for a while, better for your reputation than having cable or an Atari. Of course, MTV and games like Defender and Pac Man soon changed this. Old farm tools, old croquet sets, even stacks of old books and magazines became the currency du jour. A *Playboy* from the sixties got you three packs of baseball cards or five Hot Wheels or four comics of your choice. An old comic with a hero we knew got you one pack of cards or a five-minute ride on the latest motorized toy—moped, dirt bike, or go-kart. If only such bargains would work now…

The back alleys offered better routes than the sidewalks, which ended in weird spots and offered no resistance to the roots of the half-century old oaks that assaulted them at even intervals. The sidewalks were mainly used to show off new bike tricks picked up from *Boys Life* or *Wide World of Sports* and as raw material for spur of the moment art shows or graffiti wars on the blacktopped roads. Many a spot was marked with the blood of a young daredevil whose last words before a broken bone or busted lip were, "Hey! Y'all watch this!"

The river served mainly as a way to escape the summer heat, though it was frowned upon by parents and other authority figures. Many a kid caught his first glimpse of the opposite sex's underwear—and more—thanks to its proximity because going home with wet clothes would lead to a neighborhood-wide dragnet, searching for the ringleader with severe punishment looming for all involved. Heck, in spots, I bet the bottom is lined with underwear of all sizes, shapes, and colors.

It was also home to an abandoned flood control tower—which served as a convenient spot for sampling one's first beer, cigarette or joint, along with the joys offered by the opposite sex, if you were of an age to be worried about such—and the remnants of its dam. However, you had to remember to stay between the old dam and the shoals just upriver of the wastewater plant. Otherwise you might wind up with leeches all over your legs or find a cottonmouth to nibble on your toes. Plus, everyone knew from scouts that you could only drink running water, so it made sense to play in it too.

About a half-mile from the tower, the trestles crossed the river and the landscape changed from grassy banks with the occasional water oak or cedar to honest-to-God woods. I mean woods like those once haunted by Thoreau. I'm sure they weren't virgin woods, but the closely packed trees and eternal shade put one in that frame of mind. The wild dogs that roamed them and the rumors of moonshiners and pot growers kept you on your toes and leaning toward the trestles for a hasty escape.

For all the appeal of the forbidden tracks and out-of-bounds river, the two creeks offered the most bang for the buck, so to speak. Direct access to water, lack of pesky adult supervision, and an ever-changing host of other goodies were among the allure of the creeks.

The main one was the longer of the two, the one we all called Park Creek. It ran from the town park, which consisted of a metal slide, suitable for roasting calves and thighs through the thickest corduroy pants; a swing set that featured at least three of the four swings wrapped completely around the top bar, and the fourth always consisted of two chains hanging parallel; and the usual basketball and tennis courts.

The basketball court was basically an area of coal gravel and red mud below a hoop-less basketball goal, and the tennis court was a large rectangle of concrete marked with faded black paint and no net. We used it as a substitute Daytona or Indianapolis for large scale bike races, since the only racket sport we ever played was badminton in gym class.

The creek emerged from a grate just across the street at the foot of what seemed to us to be a cliff topped by the highway. It was all of twenty feet high and just about vertical. It ran through backyards on a meandering course through scattered trees. If you were either taller than average or very nimble, you could traverse the couple of hundred feet from the park to the highway culvert on rocks, roots, and sandbars and emerge with dry shoes or feet. Those of us who could do this quickly learned that not everybody can be taught and not everything can be taught, especially to tagalong siblings. They almost always wound up soaked from eyeballs to toenails, leading to big trouble for those of us left "in charge."

The culvert, universally known as the little tunnel, was, basically, a concrete box ten feet high and about twenty feet long and open at both ends. When a semi would pass overhead, dust and small rocks would rain down like snow in February. The only way to navigate it was to simply walk straight down the middle, throwing any chance of dry shoes to the wind because who knew what dangers lurked on the dark bottom. There could be busted bottles, rocks, or any kind of aquatic life awaiting a chance at your naked toes, which would lead to the trip to the doctor for the tetanus shot and the endless lectures to boot.

The six-inch deep water was cold year-round, which gave added incentive to keep your shoes on. The nails that had served some unknown purpose during the construction of the culvert still lurked in the concrete walls, as I discovered to my dismay one spring morning. I still have the scar, and I'm sure my mom still has the gray hair it caused. If you were afraid of the dark, the unknown or tight spaces, walking the little tunnel was a chore better suited to Hercules. In fact, I know a few kids who would have rather walked to the electric chair than walked it alone.

The little tunnel also served as a portal of sorts because the landscape changed on the other side. The bottom of the creek went from rocky to sandy. The creek went from well-kept backyards in sight of houses to the midst of an explosion of green. Kudzu and wisteria draped everything in all directions, down to the very edge of the creek. In spots, the tendrils would reach for your wading ankles like the hands of a witch from some old fairy tale. Most of the time, only dire need, like the retrieval of a lost ball or other toy, would induce us to leave the little tunnel.

The exceptions were late fall and early spring. In late fall, the town burned the kudzu back in a vain attempt to slow its growth, counting on a combination of gasoline and frost to do what nothing else could. Then the vast field became a playground for those of us willing to ruin clothes in the thick ash. Piles of ruined masonry and coal waste served as ammunition for slingshots and catapults, and as raw materials for dams never dreamed of by the Army Corps of Engineers, not to mention just plain missiles. Fallen pines and oaks, long covered by the rampant green, served as forts and secret bases and mighty castles. Long abandoned toys and balls became treasures worth real brawls over.

The winter diverted our interest from creeks until the days started getting longer and heavy coats gave way to light jackets or sweaters. Then the frost and freeze-ravaged field returned to our attention. As soon as we could stand to wear shorts, the big tunnel became our main obsession since we knew it would soon be out of reach, surrounded by its green guardian. The big tunnel earned its name. It was a ten-foot-high run of corrugated metal pipe that ran for close to a quarter mile or more. It ran under a set of four garages, two houses, crossed under two streets and was under a good eight feet of fill dirt. About a third of the way in, coming from the tiny tunnel end, it curved slightly to the right, making it impossible to see all the way through to the other end and plunging the intrepid walker into black darkness. If you were tall, you could straddle the foot-deep water and walk the length of it.

No one was really excited about walking in the water because of fears of what lurked in the darkness. Busted bottles, snakes, and lord-knows-what made it easier to risk a pulled groin than wet feet.

Another reason why the big tunnel was a cause of such concern was the tricks sound played in it. Between the traffic noises, running water, unexplained splashes in either direction just out of sight, *and* smartasses banging the sides and making ghost noises, you hardly knew what was going on. In fact, the only time I ever actually saw a child out of diapers pee himself was when me and a buddy were going through on a dare and a neighborhood stray decided to come join us. He freaked out, knocked me on my butt into the cold water, wet himself, ran crying like a baby out, and stayed inside for the rest of the weekend. Of course, for about two weeks, we called him "Piss Boy."

The big tunnel came out just this side of the railroad tracks with the two trestles about fifty feet from the road. The creek ran in the open for about ten feet, then entered another grated concrete pipe for the rest of its run to the waiting river. And that's how it was.

"What about the other creek, PawPaw?"

"What about it, Sandy?"

"You got to tell me about both of them. Like the other time. You promised, or I'll tell MawMaw."

"Fine. The other creek then. Good Lord, who spoiled you so bad, boy?"

It ran from the end of the street here under the railroad tracks and ran by the backside of the old warehouses by the old power plant. You know, right there at the new library we visit every other day across the road from it. It hit the river about a thousand feet up from there. If you look from the bridge, you can see where it comes in.

Now, this was a bit more like a real creek. Hell, it had catfish in it. Little ones, but still eatable enough if you could catch them. I never could and after the thing with the house, I never tried to. I know, I know, and I'm getting to it.

Now, the other creek was called Old House Creek because about halfway between the railroad tracks and the river, over on the river side of the creek, there was an abandoned house. It was built out of brick that had the rosy hue old handmade bricks have. Every window in the place was either broken or shot out, but the screens stayed put, rusty as they were. The roof was just two big pieces of corrugated tin fastened down with old square-head nails. The front porch had separated from the house and sagged toward the creek like the hull of a shipwreck on the Outer Banks. The wooden steps had long since rotted away, but it was only about two feet up to the rotting floor of the porch, and the porch was only about six inches from the house. The front door hung at a crazy angle, only connected by the bottom hinge. The screen door was fused to the porch half open. A few of the younger kids swore the place looked like a skull, but us middle schoolers just laughed at all that.

Of course, a house that beat up and in the middle of nowhere does attract its share of stories. We had heard that folks had been seen peeping out the windows and voices had been heard coming from it when it was empty. One kid, who had made himself famous as a liar, swore he had been chased off by a guy without a head. We decided that most of the stories could be blamed on either bums looking for a dry place to sleep it off or high school kids having grown-up fun. At any rate, a bunch of us decided we'd look into it for ourselves on Halloween. We figured, if nothing else, we'd find some free porn or some loose money lying around.

Now, we knew our folks wouldn't let us stay in some creepy old house just for fun. So we came up with a fool-proof—and idiot-proof—plan. We told our parents that we were going to the football game and then we'd stay with a buddy overnight. Of course, the buddy would tell his folks the same thing and use another kid's name. The secret was never to use a friend who your folks knew or knew his folks. That way, no call to confirm these plans and no worries about getting busted, which meant happy kids all around.

We decided to meet at the house at dark. That would give us all time to get comfortable and then see what was up. Basically, we all got dropped off at the game and walked right past the gate and into the woods behind the baseball field. Then, we crossed the bridge and walked behind the warehouses and down the creek to the house. We all had lighters, Swiss army knives, lock blade knives, flashlights, and anything else we could get into a jean jacket. I know one kid managed to get a whole six pack, and another grabbed a handful of mini-bottles. Me and another guy both had our cigarettes.

Once all six of us had gotten there, we argued for a few minutes about whether or not to crash in the house, but the drizzle that soon started settled that pretty quick. So we all piled into the living room. Three guys grabbed what had been a couch years before. Two of us grabbed pieces of the hearth in front of the fireplace we hoped didn't harbor any pets, and another guy drug an old metal drinking water tub that had washed downstream from the railroad in for a chair. The next hour or so passed as they do. One guy managed to remember his pocket radio, so we could listen to the football game, which was good because we knew we'd get quizzed about it in the morning. We trotted out our newest dirty jokes, discussed who we'd do at school or wouldn't, and traded lies about our prowess so far. You know, the usual stuff eleven and twelve-year-old boys do.

We spilt the booze; I remember having at least one beer with the Coke I had brought. Then, the fun started. Somebody asked what time it was, and I remember saying ten because the post-game show had just gone off—we lost 24-10 to guarantee us a losing record.

No sooner than the words had left my lips, we noticed one of the guys had wandered off. With a chorus of grumbles and idle threats, we decided to go hunt him and explore the rest of the house. Right off the living room was the kitchen. The wood stove and sink basin were still intact, but there wasn't a fridge. The sink didn't have a faucet, which told me that there was a well around somewhere. The doors of the cabinets were all on the floor, and the shelves were all empty. Most important, it was empty of people. So we all headed down the hall.

Sharing a wall with the living room was a small bedroom. A pile of dirty foam stuffing and rusted springs marked the spot where the bed had stood. Otherwise, the floor was a sea of beer cans, used condoms, empty wrappers, and abandoned clothes. Windows on both walls were just blank spots with no glass or screen to keep out the elements. Directly across the hall was a larger bedroom. It was marked by the same general mess of beer cans, used rubbers, torn-up magazine pages, and a pile of stuffing, rusty metal, and old sheets of some kind. The window on the side wall actually had glass in two of the eight panes, and our buddy was standing at the back window, which though completely glassless did have a rusty screen still attached. He was peeing through the screen and writing his name on it in cursive. Despite his pleas for privacy, we rained insults about the smallness of his equipment down on him, which got him all ready for a fight.

Until the house got cold and we heard the squeak of a wagon and whinny of a horse outside the front of the house. We all got quiet and everything got put back into place, and we listened intently. Every one of us was ready to dash out the non-existent back door at a dead run and the Devil take the hindmost at that point.

Then we heard a *thunk* like something had fallen onto the floor of the porch, like some firewood or something. I got "appointed" lookout and was motioned to look out toward the door. Just my head popped out of the frame the whole house shook with the *bang* of a wooden door being thrown open violently. However, the actual door still hung cockeyed as ever, and the space beyond was as empty as ever.

We then heard the oddest thing. It sounded like somebody dragging a golf club or something down a carpeted floor and it was coming our way, along with heavy footsteps, like those of a man wearing work boots. But the hallway was empty. Then, a mass of cold air, cold enough to make us see our breath, hit us all at once. We then heard a series of thuds, like somebody pounding on a desk, followed by a woman's scream.

Well, that was that. We all took off like we was in the Olympics. I hollered for everybody to come to my great-granddaddy's place because he'd lived here since the day after the mill opened, and if anybody could explain what happened, he could. We covered the three blocks in about thirty seconds, seemed like, and all piled up on his steps while I rang the doorbell.

Thankfully, great-granddaddy was still up and so was great-grandmaw. She made us all tea and a ham sandwich while we all talked at once, until he hushed us with a well-aimed stream of tobacco juice into the wood stove. He told us that the house was the old Grier home place and that it had been built by the folks who farmed the land that was now the village after the War betwixt the States, as he put it.

The last of them was an old man who had fought in the war and who couldn't make a go of it farming. He married a sweet, young thing and brought her home. Now, he was in his sixties, and she was no more than twenty. After he sold the land for the mill, the new owners hired a crew to come build it and the village. Mr. Grier still had land enough to live off of, if the weevils stayed away and the deer didn't eat more than their share.

Well, the bride was tired of living out in the sticks with this dirty old man for company. She took to hanging out at the mill site, just watching at first. Then, the foreman took notice and started to chat her up. She decided to ask her husband if the foreman could board with them for cash money since he needed to be closer to work and they could use the ready money.

With most of his crops planted on the river bottom, Mr. Grier said fine to this arrangement, but made sure the foreman knew where the line was concerning certain things.

For about a month, everything was fine. Then, the wife got a bad case of hot pants and decided to have the foreman cure them. Well, being a sensible man, he decided to help her with her problem. For another month, they had a blast. It was harvest time, and Mr. Grier and the few tenants he had were busy from dark to dark loading wagons up to carry off to the sale. Until the day he decided to quit a bit early.

Mr. Grier came home and saw the foreman's horse still tied to the porch rail. Well, Mr. Grier was trusting, but damned if he was dumb. He slid off the wagon's seat and stepped off onto the porch. In a step, he was at the woodpile and grabbed his axe. He was so blame mad by this point that he decided to make a scene, so he kicked the door in quicker than a mule in a pile of yeller jackets. He drug the axe behind him, all the while praying that he was wrong.

Then, he got to his bedroom and saw them. Together. Doing what only a man and wife should do. And that was that. He stepped into the room and went to town on them both with the axe. The first whack caught the foreman in the small of the back, and the groan he let out and the blood he spat out caused Mrs. Grier to scream bloody murder. For about three seconds, then her husband stopped her tongue good. Then Mr. Grier dropped the axe, went onto the porch, lit a cigar, and waited for his tenants to come running. He calmly sent them to fetch the local constable and waited for him. Left with the law and never spoke again until they hung him in Columbia three months later.

Well, that settled that. None of us ever went back to Old House Creek and haven't showed any sign of wanting to go back now. I've heard it burned down a few years later, but I was already in college and wasn't all that concerned.

"Thanks PaPaw. Oh, if my momma or daddy calls tonight hunting me, I'm going to the ball game with some fellas."

"That's fine, but it burned down. I'll be up just in case."

A Long Time Between Drinks

ALMOST EVERYBODY KNOWS THAT WADE HAMPTON THE THIRD "REDEEMED" South Carolina from the reputed horrors of Republican (African-American) rule in 1876 by being elected Governor. Just about that many remember that Zebulon Vance was not only War Governor of North Carolina, but was its "redeemer" as well.

Both men served in the Civil War and were well-known throughout the South in their chosen fields. Vance as a lawyer and Hampton as a planter. Of course, like Southerners of generations both before and after theirs, they were both bitten by the political bug. Our story doesn't focus on the rip-roaring days of Civil War combat or the sly maneuverings in the United States Senate, or even the thunder of oratory during a campaign for Governor. Oh no, we're more interested in a quiet moment between two old warhorses, two fellows having dinner.

"Well, Governor, that was some fine dining. Terrapin soup, deer and beef steaks, and a mess of partridges, too. And all the vegetables and the watermelon came from your garden here in Charlotte. Mercy... And the apples for the applejack and the scuppernongs for the wine, as well?"

"Yes sir, General Hampton. If the Lord allows it to be grown in the dirt and for man to use it for nourishment, it came from right here on this property. I'll show you around in the morning and see if anything catches your eye for luncheon. Now I know my garden is not the reason that brings you all the way to Charlotte from Columbia. So, let's settle accounts."

"Senator Vance, your profession betrays you. Your legal mind is too focused on business. I'm here to recollect on our three decades of public service to our states and section and to pass the time before we both go north for the special congressional session to tackle that damned tariff bill of McKinley's. I have no real axe to grind, though a mutual friend of ours did ask that you prevail upon one of your successors to return Tom Harrill Junior to South Carolina. We both know he murdered poor Reverend Robert Dixon right there in his church at Yorkville, then stole the money for the missions, and then ran off down toward Wilmington. We both also know that he should hang for I,t and since North Carolina seems to be squeamish about justice..."

"Now, Senator Hampton, how's your leg? Here, let's properly medicate it with some more of this fresh applejack, since the wine doesn't seem to be to your taste. Now, we both know that Governor Fowle is a good Christian man who hasn't liked me much since I fired him back during the war. Heck, with all the trouble that Tillman man is causing down your way, I'm surprised Governor Richardson asked you to check on it. I would have thought he'd rather send one of Tillman's friends."

"Well, Mr. Tillman and his friends seem to be far more hands-on than we ever were. Especially when it comes to law and order and maintaining white supremacy and such like. I really think Richardson is worried that if he sent a Tillmanite up here, either y'all would kill the fool or he'd kill Dixon on sight 'to spare the widow.' But I've made my informal request for you to drop by Raleigh at your leisure. Now, I do have another question for you, and this one is solely meant to soothe my curiosity. Why do the ghosts in the mountain tales always have to interact with the living? I saw an article in the *Post and Courier* of Charleston a few days ago about a man in gray seen on Pawley's Island near Governor Allston's old place just before the big earthquake, and he never acknowledged any witnesses at all, just sauntered on by like he owned the place. Meantime, I have heard servants over at High Hampton whispering about hearing the fiddle of a man who died before the war over on one of the big rock outcrops. Hence my question."

"Well, General, I don't rightly know, but I can make a guess. Most of the ghost tales down your way get told by darkies on the coast. Of course, something like a bridal party jumping off a wharf would be noticed, but folks raised to treat slaves as such would not notice the extra attention, be they living or dead. And let's be honest, folks on the coast down near Charleston and Georgetown would rather be seen and admired than anything else. Whereas folks in this section have always been hands-on. Most of the houses up in the high country and even down this way were built without the help of slaves. The fields and farms were tended the same way. Now, these same folks have tended to settle things themselves, too, like your Tillmanite might. So feeling the hand of a loved one who's passed would not be a surprise. Heck, for that matter, hearing a faithful hound years after it dies wouldn't be either. But that's just my thoughts on the subject."

"Be that as it may, Senator, it brings a thought to mind."

"What's that, pray tell?"

"Where's the jug? Because it's been a long time between drinks."

NOTE: As far as I know, the above meeting never happened. I have set it in 1890, as that was toward the end of both Vance's and Hampton's public career, and they would be more prone to reminisce at that point. The reputed origin of the line "a long time between drinks" dates from an actual meeting of North Carolina Governor J.M. Morehead and South Carolina Governor J.H. Hammond (who was Wade Hampton III's uncle) in the early 1840s to discuss the extradition of an accused murderer who fled from South Carolina to North Carolina to escape the death penalty.

The Eternal Internal Monologue

The noise from the car stereo said it all. "… **Widely scattered and** locally heavy thunderstorms are likely until dark. Basically, you may get wet, but your neighbor might not. Low sixty-two, and tomorrow, more of the same with a high of eighty. It's six p.m. and back to the…"

Just as the car pulled out into the gully-washer that decided to hammer the intersection of SC 103 and SC 104 onto 103 toward Hemphill with a squeal of wet rubber on wet asphalt, a little spot of ground fog and road spray coalesced into a humanoid shape that swayed gentle against the light breeze.

"…ercy! Damn… how long have I been out? And sooo-wee what a dream. Lemme see what time it is.

(Pulls battered silver watch face from his shirt pocket and drops it at his feet.)

Sixish? Cool, I have time to make it over to Gene's Pool Hall before they runs out of the two dollar big beers in the cold can. Hey, is that LeRoi Hughes coming? Better flag him down, since he owes me twenty bucks from the Super Bowl. Damnit, wave back, you old fool!

(Despite his best efforts, both arms remain firmly at his sides as he sways against the heavier breeze of a semi.)

Watch out! Damned fool acted like I was invisible and almost nicked me with his bummer.

(Bends at waist and checks his reflection in a nearby puddle, then staggers forward. He lands in the center of the puddle, and the muddy, reddish-brown water floods into his ripped-up, worn out sneakers. Despite this, his stained and battered mesh and cloth baseball cap with the bill split in two never teeters.)

Naw, I ain't invisible yet, but I could damn well be bulletproof. And purty, wee-ooo, you knows it! Hmm, I best call my boy Ephus and make sure he's bringing me back to the house. Damned sure don't wanna dance with any loggin' trucks tonight. Now, which pocket is it in?

(Despite his best efforts at patting himself down, again, his arms never move.)

Huh… must have left it at the house. Oh well, if Ephus is like his old man, he's already there and eyeing the gal behind the counter. I'll ax him when

I get there. Lord, sure is plenty enough traffic today. Must be a ball game or somethin'. Shame I can't find no kind, sweet soul to give me a ride tho'. I shore hate all that walkin, 'specially when I get a bit tipsy. Least 103 is pretty flat. Hate those hills 'tween here and Pickneyville. Welp, time to head out.

(The figure takes three steps into the south-bound lane of Highway 104, two angling north and one angling southwest, and throws his arms up in front of his face.)

Lord! Forgive me! Never even seen him a-coming atal. Have M—"

With that, the intersection returns to its usual slow pace with few cars crossing and most of the drivers never giving Highway 103 a second thought... until next year.

ON THE NUPTIALS AT KASSEL KLIRREN...

I ARRIVED AT THE KLIRRENBERG ON THE RIVER BANNO TO INVESTIGATE THE rumored disruptions of castle routine by various supernatural means in advance of the wedding of Lachlan, the thirty-first Duke of Rotenerde—an old chum from University—and his intended, Ekaterina, the Comtesse de Casgente, on a fall day that would be called dreary by anyone not native to the East End of London.

The sky was a gray unseen in nature outside of the waters of the Thames at flood. The clouds reached from the very vault of Heaven to the gravel of the well-kept road, not that our driver even noticed or slowed his blistering pace, despite a lack of visibility I have not seen outside the Harz or Carpathians much less on flat land like the valley of the Banno. If not for the occasional chime of a church bell dolefully marking the passage of time or the shout of a fisherman, one would have thought we had passed into another world, out of time and more home to fairy folk than Anglo-Saxons.

Thankfully, the horns of the passing boats and tinkle of ferry bells served to remind both us and our driver of the closeness of the river as the road ran almost at the edge of the bank from the station at Wohnberg to the gatehouse of the Berg. The fact that it was known as the widest road in Europe between Berlin and Moscow and ran almost straight also helped overcome any qualms as to our driver's skill. I was accompanied by my young research assistant—and nephew of the Home Secretary and some degree of cousin to the groom—Sir Rodney Walthgate, the third son and heir of the Earl of Seaforth, and by my most trusted servant and body man, a veteran of Afghanistan, China, and the Sudan with the (late) Prince of Wales Own 27th Hussars named Long Will Shefford who stood six-foot-ten in his stocking feet and could straighten five horseshoes at once without a sweat. He was a very handy man to have around in case of any physical activity, which I try to avoid as below my station.

I had decided in the interest of discretion to limit my party to a minimum, trusting on my host to provide any other servants and thanked the lord for the use of English as a court tongue thanks to our grand Protestant heritage and for the power of the Pound to overcome silly superstition.

After arriving safely at the Berg and paying our driver his outlandish fare, even I as I thanked him for his daredevil skill for breaking the monotony of the long train journey from Paris to Berlin to Wohnberg. I even more eagerly awaited the bliss of good food, good quality company, and clean sheets.

Due to the lateness of our arrival—it was approaching dark—my party and I decided to eat a light four-course meal and then to retire, but only after I had sent my card to the Duke's vizier, an expatriate Irishman named Brumley, late in the service of the Duchess of Sheerson, the Comtesse's late mother, with hopes of meeting him after breakfast to get a feel for the lay of the land and to see what my next moves should be.

From the few credible press reports I had found, the families of both the Duke of Rotenerde and the Comtesse de Casgente had multiple harbingers of family doom, death, or bad luck that dated back through the various branches and line all the way to Charlemagne. The usual stew of European royalty, great and small, Protestant and Catholic, bubbled in their veins, blending Cornish and Slav, Scot and Breton, Welsh and Dane into a mosaic of fame and infamy. All these were coated with the veneer of Saxe-Gotha probity and Hapsburg romance.

Tales of female specters clad in every hue of the rainbow, both with and without heads, stalking every corridor of Klirrenberg while everything from headless hounds to wingless birds filled the grounds to capacity allowed the more unscrupulous press to engage in flights of fancy unseen since the days of Napoleon. They also cast a pall over the joyous coming occasion deeper than the illness of the groom's father, the Margrave of Askanlp and Prince-Elector or Ossray, the severity and duration, not to mention the cause, of which had so far conquered the greatest medical minds from across Europe.

The Duchess of Sheerson's rather cryptic comments about the cause and nature of the Margrave's illness, coupled with the impending wedding of her daughter with the thoroughly Anglophile Duke—and possible future Holy Roman Emperor should anything come of the current uproar in Berlin about deposing Kaiser Frederick the Third and reinstating the Empire as many expect due to the growing instability of the Kaiser and his likely heir—have not reduced the public's appetite for news from Klirrenberg, either truthful or fanciful. The recent announcement in the Commons by the Conservative leader, Lord Marlborough, that he would call "for a thorough investigation of our relations with the German states, especially concerning the security of guests at Klirrenberg and the recent discussions in the Reichstag" if his party carries the election next year was the impetus for my visit to evaluate the controversies firsthand and recommend any needed action to the Cabinet and to the Prime Minister, Lord Harcourt.

After a fairly restful night, not having heard the steady trod of hob-booted peasants in some manner of procession that apparently disturbed Rodney's rest, and having a light breakfast of four poached eggs, a rasher of broiled bacon, a half loaf of fresh baked bread with local wild grape jam, as well as coffee and porter, my party and I met with Brumley in his tiny makeshift office in the jailer's office of the castle's long-disused dungeon. His shock of steadily retreating and uncontrolled white hair, and his breath, stinking of garlic and day old beer, were the only signs that he was present behind a raft of wedding invitation responses and mounds of more mundane paperwork.

"Well, I am always happy to assist any agent of Her Majesty since that is where my main loyalty will always lie, but I am afraid that I just do not understand your brief. Since when are sorry peasant lies and jealous rumors of any interest to anyone with a bit of sense in London?"

"Well, suffice it to say, they are interested almost as much as they are for any hard news from Berlin. Whether or not it is just titillation or there is a practical purpose is not for me to judge. All I do is provide the data, and Special Branch and all the rest will do the analysis. I have heard from Sir Rodney that some peasants on parade in boots interrupted his slumber last night, though I was undisturbed at the far end of the corridor. What other manner of foolishness should we expect?"

"Honestly, I think Barnum should set a stand up out front. At a pfennig or two a head, he'd make enough to buy a dozen Feejee Mermaids. The whole thing smacks of hokum, superstition and the barnyard, to be polite. But let me see… I have a specially commissioned illuminated genealogy of both the families of the bride and the groom with a history of the Kassel as well… if I can excavate it from these mounds of trivia.

(Two large piles of invoices fall to the bare stone floor with a thud that echoes back to us through the deserted dungeon as he pulls an enormous book the size of two large Exchequer ledgers joined end to end from under them. The cover is a color engraving of the two families' coats-of-arms joined, done in the best style of a Rossetti, Burne-Jones, or Morris, if not from their own hand, with a black line engraving of the Kassel behind.)

"Hmmm… if I can decipher this Gothic scribble, we'll see what's what. Why the Devil they didn't just typeset the thing. Ah, here it is. Legends of the Past… Let's see, we have a Blue Lady here at the Kassel, the groom's family has a phantom coach with headless coachman and a banshee, as well, and the bride has a spectral raven that appears outside any sickroom when the patient is doomed. The poet, Myers, and the chemist, Crookes, and their crew would have a blast with this drivel.

(After a withering glance from me, his grin vanished.)

"But there it is. Now, as far as any guests go… Oh, and the Duke has said he eagerly awaits your company for luncheon at one today. You'll be dining al fresco, however."

"I think those should be our main foci for now. Is there any chance of having the relevant pages of that tome copied by one of your assistants by dinner this evening? I am quite sure that Rodney would not mind assisting in this endeavor and no harm will come to the document, of course. Her Majesty would be thankful, as will I.

(Here I ran my fingers along the lapel of my jacket, making a clear implication of the form my appreciation would take.)

"I thank you for your time, and please inform the Duke that I will be prompt in my attendance."   ·

With that, I concluded the interview, leaving Rodney in my wake to finalize the price of my copies and to hopefully extract more useful information from Brumley. I did not care a continental for the cost since I had my own means, and the Prime Minister had already assured me of prompt repayment for any expenses.

I spent the intervening time in the castle's rather sparse for its age library trying to fill in the background of the limited knowledge Brumley added to my store. Sadly, between Gustavus Adolphus and Napoleon, very little prior to the Congress of Vienna, at which it was decided that the Margrave of Alkanalp and the Prince-Elector of Ossray would be named Emperor-Elect if the two titles were ever helped by the same person and if the peoples of Greater Germany through the Prussian Reichstag and Austrian Diet decided to revive the Holy Roman Empire.

The document stating this, though an engrossed copy and not the original, which still resided in the archives of the Hapsburgs, held pride of place under a portrait of the first Duke of Rotenerde in full armor. Thankfully, I expected to see it and made a mental note to have my sources in London verify the veracity of the document versus the copy of the minutes of the Congress in the holdings of the Foreign Office.

Just after noon, Sir Rodney rejoined me in the library, effusive in his praise of "kind Bardolph" and his "tender solicitation." After determining that a large part of Brumley's kindness was administered via a syringe full of a three percent solution of morphia and cocaine, as well as other things not to be put on paper, I resolved to have Long Will visit Brumley to remind him of the proper way to entertain an English gentleman. However, after administering some direct means to counter the poison, I did learn that Brumley had been the primary source of the leaks of the reported supernatural incidents due to his disdain for life in rural Mittel Europa as opposed to Caledonia and to an apparent influx of capital from persons unknown in Berlin.

In my own opinion of the man, I thought him to be a cynic and a skeptic with both eyes on the main chance and loyalty only to himself. Rodney also informed me that our copy of the genealogy would be ready for perusal after our luncheon and offered to go fetch it himself, but I insisted that Long Will go, both to perform the task mentioned above and out of concern that our mutual friend, Lachlan, would keep us overlong at his leisure. And, sure enough, that was indeed the case.

Sir Rodney and I arrived at the Grecian-style combination folly and waterfowl blind named the Chram of Sior just outside the main channel of the Banno just as Duke Lachlan was firing off the dregs of his third box of shells of the morning. On a barge about five hundred yards from us, we saw the fruits of his labors—ducks and woodcocks piled five or six deep with four Jack Russell Terriers in the water bringing yet more in.

Just at the end of the flagstone paved path ahead of us and just inside the wrought-iron gate, a crook-backed, wizened fellow was raking mounds of spent shells and dead soldiers into the river willy-nilly. He was heard to remark over and over in some odd Slavic tongue, "lillad, lillad," which we later understood to refer to the profusions of violets in bloom on the riverside, which struck us as curious given the season.

The Duke had learned to shoot at the feet of several master marksmen and expert huntsmen, including his distant relation the Duke of York, and the results showed that, as did his joviality and grace when he greeted us.

We dined on fresh fried fish, oaten bread, steam river mussels, and a brace of fried quail that had been on the wing just an hour before. The local stout—

that rivaled anything to be found in London—apricot brandy, and wild grape wine flowed in torrents only rivaled by the waters passing by us. The duke looked as happy and rested as he had been since our last meeting just prior to our farewell dinner at the Middle Temple a decade before.

Then, the tall, slender redhead with the thickest brogue south of the Orkneys had left a trail of broken hearts and shattered hymens throughout the United Kingdom and most of the Continent as well, not to mention a ledger book's worth of gaming debts from Bath to Monte Carlo and back. Now, the red hair had faded somewhat and no longer descended past his collar. The streaks of gray at each temple, along with a scattering of laugh lines and crow's feet, gave his once sallow and rather ordinary face new character that befitted his new rank and maturity. His hazel eyes were clear and matched well his bushy eyebrows. His nose was Roman and straight, but showed a hint of dissipation in the redness it displayed at all seasons.

At six-foot-three, the duke towered over both Sir Rodney and me by at least four inches each. His slender build was well displayed in his bespoke Saville Row suits. Only his cravat offered any hint of color in his attire. He detested hats in all weather and insisted on tucking his slacks into his knee-high riding boots.

In his religion, his family was Presbyterian from the days of Knox, but he was far from a zealot, insisting only that he be allowed to worship as he saw fit and that every other man was entitled to the same courtesy. As a student, both at the Temple and at University, he was indifferent, mainly focused on the social life but showing some skill in politics and in the study of history. He had no problem with Latin, but the passing of Greek required the help of several tutors. Like most of us, he trusted in his titles and in his father's trust fund for his future.

He served as a Conservative from Lerwick in the Commons for two sessions while completing his studies at the Middle Temple until the passage of the second reform bill killed the pocket borough and would have made Lachlan face the public in a place he'd never seen. Despite my being a Liberal Member from Cochrane-on-Helford, our friendship was unharmed, since we only attended at the Opening and when our Party's Whip required it, much like I have in the Lords since.

His selection as the new Duke of Rotenerde by its citizens following the hasty abdication of the previous duke following the antics of his twin fourteen-year-old mistresses stunned all of us. Especially given that Rotenerde was thought to be a Catholic stronghold due to its strategic location on the rear flank of the Prussian Empire and proximity to the cauldron of the Balkans. Then we acknowledged that the income from the Duchy would be sufficient, along with his trust, to pay off all his debts and stifle any lingering domestic unhappiness, like his low-born mistresses. The change to a Protestant family was not an obstacle, since it merely resorted the balance between the faiths in the Germanies.

After a wandering chat about the latest gossip in our circle and goings-on throughout the capitals of the Continent, not to mention the lack of available… afterhours entertainment on hand, I decided to take advantage of the arrival of the third pitcher of stout since the end of lunch to breach the real reasons for my visit to Klirren besides the coming nuptials.

"Well, Your Grace, as you doubtless know, Sir Rodney and I have a tri-fold purpose to this visit. Besides your eagerly awaited wedding and our long separation, we need some intelligence on your intentions concerning the crown of Charlemagne for the Cabinet, assuming the worst and your father does not assume it as well as on the rumored supernatural events reported in the penny press. I'll dispense with formalities and just ask: do you intend to accept the crown of the Holy Roman Emperor from the Reichstag, failing that, will you insist on a regency under your father's name? I ask only for a gut reaction, man to man. I trust you to write up any formal declaration of your feelings at your pleasure."

"Well, I would reject the crown faster than you could say 'Jack Robinson.' The post would be as ceremonial as the American Presidency and as full of potential dangers as being the doorman of the Grand Turk's harem. All this is putting aside the Prussian insistence that they fight a war against someone every few years and the Austrian dread of any change more lasting than a change of undergarment. In short, I would swap my life here for a routine full of bored courtiers and a view of a sewer. I'd rather carry coals to Newcastle or cotton to Charleston. Besides, anyone fool enough to think that the Prussians will give the power they've spent all these years, not to mention the blood and iron, accumulating on the say-so of a half-dozen princelings, is in for a real wake up call.

"Now I think there is a better chance we Brits will give India to the Tsar for Christmas this year than of me ever being Holy Roman Emperor. I know that the P.M. will not be thrilled to hear that, but they are, frankly, stuck with the Prussians, and I would advise them to pressure Wilhelm to set up a regency-in-waiting as soon as the Reichstag reburies the Empire. Frederick's mental state is not promising, and the Prussian people want resources and space and will fight to get them, mark my words. I can see a repeat of Sedan coming and would advise the Cabinet to go with the victors. Not to mention, any continental adventures will limit the mischief they cause our interests in Africa and Asia. In fact, one of my dinner guests will be of interest to you. He is a true believer of a Junker named Von Hissler who serves in the Reichstag and is very friendly with both the Kaiser and the Crown Prince. He is rumored to be either the bastard or the morganatic son of Ludwig of Bavaria. With his connections, you may get a better view of things in Berlin than our Minister has."

"Well, damnation, I had so wanted to be a Knight of the Holy Roman Empire when I grew up. I'll settle for the Garter one of these days. But now, what about this ghost nonsense? Brumley showed us the musty tome one of your maiden American aunts excavated for a wedding gift. According to the genealogical gobbledegook in it, you, your intended, and the Kassel itself all have either a family ghost or some manner of death omen. Have you even ever heard any of these stories, much less had any encounters with the other side?"

"Let's see…I have heard that before my grandfather, the first Margrave, passed away in Spain while with Wellesley that a jet-black coach pulled by four headless horses driven by a man in Cavalier garb with his head in his lap—some witnesses said it was Charles the First, himself. Both headed across plowed fields and through walls and stiles, finally coming upon the main drive at Askanalp at a full run on the night before reputed bandits, but more likely French troops, prior to the battle at Barrosa ambushed Grandfather's unit. He was stabbed in the back seven times with a bayonet of French manufacture, so draw your own conclusions.

"The survivors reported to my grandmother that at dusk of the fatal day, a strange female voice was heard keening and wailing in a dialect unknown in the country but that sounded vaguely Celtic or Gaelic. They heard only one recognizable word, which was his given name of Allan, but no one ever saw a thing. I really can't speak for the Comtesse, but I have heard that when her father was on his deathbed, a raven with a clipped wing and an oddly askew beak alighted on the sill of the bay window in his bedroom, pecking at the glass and slapping at the panes with its good wing like it sought entry. It showed up just after the doctor declared his case hopeless of recovery and hung about until after the burial.

"About a week later, a workman sent to replace a cracked pane in the same window made mention of the fact that the sill was so narrow he could not set a scraper down without risking it falling some twenty odd feet to the ground. He also mentioned when asked that he saw no sign of any bird having been on the sill at all. Hmm... At Roebourne Manor, my birthplace, we are only bedeviled by lazy servants and inattentive tenants, but no things that go bump in the night.

"One of the grooms here at Klirren told me that the Berg is haunted by the former mistress of a long-dead duke who was famed locally for both her love of blue watered silk gowns and tendency to brag out of turn about her lover's abilities and deficiencies in equal measure. When he tired of both her well-worn favors and slashing tongues, he settled the latter by biting most of her tongue off and stabbing her privates with his saber after a final embrace at the foot of the grand staircase. She fled upstairs, grabbing with equal fervor at her crotch and her mouth, trying in vain to scream to summon assistance, only to collapse dead on the fifteenth stair.

"Before the marble stairs were carpeted after the final defeat of Napoleon, numerous guests complained at the infernal slickness of that step and the odd coloration it sported compared to its fellows. The odd coloration, which seems to have been a pinkish-gray in contrast to the bluish-gray on the others, led the servants to believe it was the mistress's blood eternally showing her lover's guilt, especially since no chemical compound seemed to affect the stain at all. Rumors have it that a passing Gypsy prince prescribed a solution for the stain involving wolfbane and dollops of black magic, but I think he simply saw a chance to sell some Berber carpet at a premium.

"Ah, I bet you haven't even noticed that rock pile on the far bank. Well, though it has nothing to do with me, it's an interesting tale all the same. Back in the days of the Teutonic Knights, a young man was out smuggling some pagans across the Banno one moonlit night. At the moment the last stragglers hit the water, a roar of hunting horns shattered the still night air. Better than a dozen hounds descended onto the poor souls in the water, devouring at least three children in a twinkling of an eye. The huntsmen followed, slashing and stabbing wildly and felling a half-dozen more. Our brave smuggler emerged from his warren on the riverbank to stop the slaughter and was immediately turned to stone.

"Now, on moonlit summer nights near the solstice when the air does not stir, a black hound is seen wandering that dirt track there. Any who encounter his blazing crimson eyes will die within the year. Now the hunters leave any game killed on the track at the standing stone called the Paserak in an attempt to distract the beast from its mission.

"Oh, before you fellows escape to your own devices, let me make mention that Ekaterina will be here by supper and she has wired ahead her delight at seeing you both, but begs your indulgence if she takes the remains of the day to recover and rest. She did mention perhaps a meeting after breakfast in the morn. Now…if you will excuse me, I will see you at supper."

With that, Lachlan left us and returned to the Kassel to change from his shooting togs and into his judicial attire since he had to hold manorial court this afternoon and arbitrate some petty feud between two peasant families over the rights to a hog or some such stuff and nonsense. The sweeper reminded us that dinner would be at seven and would be formal. He also made a leering mention of the bachelor bacchanalia to follow in the riverside grottos beyond the castle walls downriver.

Sir Rodney and I thanked him for the information and returned to our rooms to change and to prepare letters for London with our news. On the way, Sir Rodney remarked that he had overheard some servants conversing in some pseudo-Slavic patois of which the only intelligible word was "geist," which as we both knew from experience was German for ghost. But we wrote it off as the babble of superstition and the ignorance of peasants. If only we had not…

After compiling our news about Lachlan's dim view of the resurrection of the Empire and his General Sherman-esque refusal of the throne in any event into dispatch form for delivery via special messenger, we received two telegrams of note while at the station in Wohnberg.

The first, from Alkanalp, informed of the margrave's rapidly declining condition, his life was moving peacefully toward its close, and the end was days, if not hours, away. It also asked that Lachlan not be informed until after the wedding, as it was considered bad luck to be married in mourning dress.

The second was from our minister in Berlin who told us that the Reichstag had rudely refused to entertain the delegates from Austria and their resolution concerning the revival of the Empire. The Reichstag also denied the Centre Party's call for a Regency for Frederick, claiming his health was "extraordinary" and that the Crown Prince thought the idea smacked of treason. The one bright spot from our immediate perspective was a mention of the loyalty and discernment of our host to the true heirs of Frederick the Great and Charlemagne.

Needing to digest this rather large stock of information, Rodney and I decided to retire for a brief sabbatical in our chambers, though he did make mention of the need to instruct the domestics not to use so much turpentine in their cleaning before we parted.

I decided first to locate the willing wench who had evinced some interest in wiling away some hours in pleasure earlier. I found her getting corrected by a senior maid for some minor discretion with more force than the occasion called for and intervened by calling for her to prepare a bath for me in my ante-chamber. I knew her appreciation would be soon forthcoming.

She was a brunette with small teats but hips that bespoke some experience of the ways of Venus. She was tall, her gaze almost met mine, and slender. Her hair, though piled into a practical bun, was as clean as the rest of her and tokened well for avoiding the French pox, especially given her duties at the Kassel and the sizable number of guests due in.

I decided to take advantage of her indebtedness to me by asking her to play Amphitrite to my Poseidon in the large claw-foot tub in my ante-chamber, knowing that no superior would question her absence given my summons and salvation earlier. She took to the role like a born actress or fallen woman, and I was quite pleased with her performance. So pleased, in fact, that I completely forgot Rodney and Brumley's likely interlude under the baleful influence of Ganymede and whatever substances the elder man had handy down in the bowels of the Kassel.

After a delightful, though messy, hour or so tour through the garden of Helga's delights, I dismissed her with instructions to inquire as to my health after dinner and whenever it was convenient. In return, I assured her of my deep devotion and joy at our rendezvous and eagerness for a repeat performance and that I would seek to have her assigned to my chamber exclusively by the housekeeper as soon as I could.

After she finally left and I had managed to dress for dinner, Long Will came by and delivered some curious news. A massive number of stoats, hares, weasels, and huge flocks of ravens, nightjars, whippoorwills, magpies, assorted native owls, and crows all with odd markings and habits had been seen in several different and widely separated spots on the grounds. The truly disconcerting thing was the creatures' lack of response to the onslaught of expert huntsmen and sentries by way of nets, long arms, and shouts.

I jovially condemned his failure to bag any real evidence, threatening to inform his old colleagues under arms and the like. Due to the research I had done prior to this journey and some half-coherent, long repressed racial memory, I shuddered visibly at the sheer number of likely death omens present due to the types of beasts present. Hell, they probably outnumbered the total guest list due to the long-term intermarriage among the petty nobility of Europe over the long centuries past.

However, I resolved not to be the purveyor of ill tidings, but to be the most gallant amongst a veritable galaxy of my peers. To my surprise, the dining room had been completely reconfigured since breakfast. Two long tables stretched the length of the hall to seat the guests who had already arrived divided by gender while the wedding party, with the exception of the bride, whose arrival was delayed by weather, but at whose insistence the dinner continued, was seated on a raised dais at the far end. Between the two guest tables stood several smaller tables that audibly groaned under their loads.

Courses came in waves to rival those on a stormy sea and the fauna required must have depopulated most of the countryside of anything edible to the third generation. But a party such as ours made ample time to converse and flirt between themselves. I was seated next to Herr Doktor Von Hissler, which I am sure was completely unaccidental, much like the willingness of my chambermaid to entertain me so long earlier.

The doktor was surgeon to a regiment of Hussars and, if he was indeed a bastard of one of the mad Kings of Bavaria, the eccentricity and flightiness of that line had completely skipped him like a fire clearing a road. Von Hissler was more Junker than the Crown Prince and Count Bismarck combined. The only thing to come close to his priggish unyielding belief in his own natural supremacy in my experience was a run-in with a handful of followers of General Booth in the East End after a hard night of drunken carousing. Who knew "holy rollers" would use such language? But to resume my account of my chat with my new Prussian friend...

"Bosh! Geists...ghosts are nothing but fiction, fairy stories to scare kinder and old maids. They are formed from a too rich diet and too lax education. A bit more of the birch would squelch most of this ghost nonsense. Notice no proper Prussian has ever seen a ghost...only weaklings would admit such."

Obviously, he had not heard of the White Lady of the Hohenzollerns at the Berliner Schloss...his beau ideal of true Prussians, and I've learned you don't argue with a resident of Bedlam.

"An utter waste. It's almost as big a joke as the babble from Berlin about deposing our beloved Kaiser and reviving the rotten corpse of the Holy Roman Empire. I do believe that the only thing Voltaire and I agree on is that it was neither holy, Roman, nor an Empire. You'd do as well to have a black African try to run Prussia from Paris. Hell, we have just firmly put those silly Austrians in their proper place at our heels. Why would we dig up a husk to put one of them on the imperial throne, much less one more British than German?"

Here, he did toss in an apology for any insult to the duke, in what I thought was a very half-hearted manner, but the duke merely nodded politely and waved. I do believe he thought the fellow to be drunk. With that, the duke arose soon after the decanters had made one lap of the table.

"Ladies and gentlemen, I believe dessert will soon be served, and I welcome you to enjoy the Kassel's entertainments and, for the gentlemen, we will be reassembling in the billiard room. Dr. Ravensby has promised an autographed copy of his life's work for a wedding gift and then we will have other entertainment, including good Kentucky bourbon and nineteen-year-old single malt. Now, if you please..."

Ah yes, the famed Doctor Saunders Ravensby, noted author of *Coprophilia*, a very weighty tome that argues that every advance in civilization since Adam has been about separating man from his excrement and that, in order to achieve true perfection, man needs to reverse the trend. Hell, I'd rather read Erasmus Darwin's love poetry on plants, but it is rumored the good doctor is very deeply involved into the worlds of weird cults and black magic and no one wants to tempt fate.

Honestly, I would rather skip the presentation and the unavoidable speech and move directly into the real after dinner entertainment featuring Mistress Lady Olivia, the mistress of the birch, and her best pupils, but it is not my bachelor party.

The presentation was remarkably brief, given the good doctor's tendency to be prolix when in the arms of Bacchus. The only sour note was struck when a servant informed His Grace that the iron hoops on the six barrels of Malmsey he had just received as a wedding gift from one of his tenants on the Border had just fallen off the barrels, though the barrels were sound. Rodney and I acknowledged this news with knowing glances. The entertainment provided by the students of Mistress Olivia is sadly not fit to be mentioned in these pages, though I shall treasure the memories and bruises forever.

Remembering my aquatic adventures earlier, I directed Sir Rodney to remain with Long Will, discreetly present to prevent him wandering to Brumley's doubtful ministrations, and returned to my chamber, having first rescued my playmate from a lengthy round of Lutheran piety with a promise of an appearance by Priapus in her presence and person.

After a simply delightful interlude of carnal bliss of over an hour's duration, to which I credit the local wines, my nymph returned to her preparations for the morrow, and I embraced night's sinuous person.

Sadly, I was not to pass a peaceful night. I, myself, heard the tattoo of drums banging a marital air, a whining scream of a mourning female in pain, the howling of packs of hounds larger than any hunt in Britain, and an incessant ticking in the walls that cost me a new watch.

Arising at least twice to answer a booming, rapid, urgent summons upon my chamber door did not help my rest improve any. Even if I had taken a draught strong enough to conquer the cacophony outside, the atmosphere that laid upon me like a blanket of bear fur and the freezing temperature that put me in mind of winter in the Shetlands, rather than a German autumn, would have still cost me my slumber.

So when Long Will reported at breakfast that the pikesmen on ceremonial guard duty in the Sopron Tor had seen candles flickering outside windows overlooking the moat and river about a hundred feet above the nearest exterior wall, untouched by human or mortal hands, and they had heard the voice of a woman crying out a phrase over and over in a tongue no one present recognized in addition to the tuneless drumming and the howling of unseen hounds. By this point, I would not have been shocked to have seen the antlers of Herne the Hunter pass by my chamber window as plainly as if I were back at Windsor.

I did, however, hope that our newly arrived hostess and the duchess-to-be had passed a more restful night after the travels, but I knew I would soon find out firsthand. Long Will also reported that Rodney had not slipped off to meet Brumley, but had spent over an hour after my departure chatting with both Doktors Von Hissler and Ravensby. He could not determine the topics covered, but the trio seemed to be getting along famously. They left together, and Will thought they were going to continue the chat in Ravensby's chambers given that he had a full chemical laboratory installed and Rodney's intense interest. Long Will then joined the soldiers in the Tor out of a lingering sense of duty and due to my guest.

After thanking Will for his diligence, I made use of the remains of the morning to answer telegrams. Nothing unexpected arrived to change my view of the situation, though I expected my luncheon date with the duchess-to-be would do that in spades.

I met Ekaterina in her chamber for a light luncheon of local fish, fried in local ale, and pumpernickel crumbs. The Comtesse was as lovely as I recalled from our first meeting at the margrave's sixtieth birthday party at Baden some years before. Her curly, reddish-blond hair fell over her shoulders and set off her luminous blue eyes and pale skin, perfect without resort to modern cosmetics. If I had been in Lachlan's shoes, I dare say I would have immured her in the Tor until the wedding lest someone steal her away. She began our interview after we ate over Irish coffee, in my case, with more Irish than coffee in my mug.

"Well, the duke and I met in Baden some months prior to his father's birthday while we were both taking the waters. We stayed in touch, nursing the slender thread of attraction through the distractions of life and the onslaught of his other suitors. I bided my time, trusting, like Penelope, that he would remain faithful and unravel his skein in memory of me. And I patiently awaited the proposal I knew would soon come, for a woman knows long before the man such things. With the growing…unease over the antics of Kaiser Frederick and the rapid decline in the health of the margrave, our mothers decided that a prospective Protestant Holy Roman Emperor needed to have a bride to reassure any doubters of the prospect for a succession. So, expediency and true love joined forces *with* politics for once. The affairs of the heart and the affairs of state were in sync for the first time since Victoria met Albert."

Here, I must confess to not disabusing Ekaterina of her belief in the duke's faithfulness in her absence, as a gentleman, out of regard for her feelings, and in the interests of the British Empire.

"I hate to disturb your recollection, but I do need to ask. Does your family have any especial omens or ancestral ghostly legends?"

"Ah, harbingers of doom, eh? Ha, ha…there are so many. Napoleon, Metternich, Alexander of the Russias…but you mean the supernatural ones, of course. We have a bird, I believe it is a cardinal, that taps its beak and beats its wings on the window of a dying Casgente's room. If the poor soul is out of doors, then a flock of seven wild geese are heard flying over, making a peculiar whistling honking call, but they are not seen, even on clear days.

"I'm sure you recall the tales of the death of my brother, the Comte de Durville, while he was in Mexico with the Emperor Maximilian. That the firing squad was interrupted in their preparations by the honking of geese in a clear sky twice before some bandit grabbed a bayonet and simply stabbed him in the belly like a common street fighter. *Ah...*

"At any rate, we also have a boy of fourteen or so who knocks thrice on the sick chamber door. If the door is opened before the third knock, he appears wrapped in mystic flame with staring, though unseeing, eyes while the blood gushes from his throat, which has been cut from ear to ear. If this gory spectacle is seen, the patient will recover. If the fatal third knock comes, heard or not, the patient will die within the hour.

"Supposedly, the figure of the boy dates from the Massacre of Saint Bartholomew's Day when a Casgente ancestor was trapped in Paris and betrayed to the mob by a hired footman. As the mob closed in, intent on blood, the Comte slashed the informer's throat with his dagger. The poor, misguided child fell face first into the nearby fireplace and bled to death, unable to scream in his final throes of agony. The mob took the vengeance the boy could not, of course.

"But, no, I've never seen or heard anything myself worth the mentioning. Now, if you will excuse me, I need to make final preparations for the ceremony tomorrow. I fully expect and demand both a kiss and a dance at the reception."

"Of course, and I thank you for your consideration and time, my lady."

With that, I left Ekaterina and her ladies to continue their planning. While I rambled through the Kassel, I did not locate my water nymph of the previous night, to my dismay, but I did come across Von Hissler in the library. Despite my best efforts at silence, I was overheard and forced into a lengthy conversation, if you can call listening to a diatribe a conversation. A sovereign nation using submarines to fight a war in preference to dreadnoughts? Bah! It is as likely we'll use airships in the next war. These Prussians and their love of all things martial...

The remainder of my day was spent in preparation of the night's festivities, namely the wedding rehearsal and the dinner to follow. All these events proceeded without any mishap, man-made or supernatural, and everyone was in high spirits and eagerly anticipated the nuptials to come. Well, until that night.

The first uncanny event was the matter of the coaches. Myself, Sir Rodney and Von Hissler had lingered into the wee hours of the morning in the billiard room playing a rubber or two at whist and sampling more apricot brandy following dinner. However, none of us had imbibed enough to adversely affect our facilities. The two coaches outside the main entry caught our attention due to the lack of any attendants and an odd flickering coming from within.

As we closed to within ten feet of the equipages, we all noticed to a man that all the horses were headless. However, as soon as Von Hissler let slip a mumbled "Mein Gott!" both coaches and horses all vanished like ice in a cup of tea in July. We barely had time to regain our composure as the two ten-foot-high oaken doors of the main entry flew open, and we were nearly trampled from behind by a coach and four driven by a figure in black crepe who was headless as his team.

It dashed through the hall and up the grand staircase at a full gallop, only to vanish with a stink of sulfur. No sooner had it vanished than a lady dressed the style popular during our Regency ran up the same staircase grabbing at her throat while casting alternating malevolent and beseeching looks our way until she, too, disappeared at about the same spot as the coach and four.

I must confess to have not bothered to count the number of stairs she mounted. Screams and poundings from upstairs brought us back to what remained of our senses, and we flew towards the ruckus, walking sticks and jackknives at the ready.

As we rounded the corner towards our bedchambers, we were confronted by a lady in a white gown with regal mien and black holes where her eyes should have been leading a group of four faceless men in the uniform of Swiss Guards carrying a plain, wooden coffin surmounted by a ducal crown.

As soon as Sir Rodney found enough voice to challenge the macabre party, the group vanished into the far wall of the corridor without a backward glance. This development led to a general failing of nerve for the entire party, so we all dashed pell-mell for the nearest room, which happened to be Von Hissler's.

Frau Von Hissler slept on through our entry and all the events before and after, barely flinching at any noise louder than her snores, which were very healthy.

Upon finding safe ground, we three compared notes and tried to determine what was next. At this point, we all got an additional scare when the chamber door was flung open. Thankfully, it was just Long Will, who had been checking both Sir Rodney's and my chambers with news, entering at a dead run.

The grounds were alive with all manner of weasels, stoats, and hares, none of whom could withstand close scrutiny or the bark of long arms without simply melting into nothingness. The keening cries of a woman in deathly pain and of a lady searching fruitlessly for something or someone echoed off the stone walls both inside and out even as we talked in whispers. The odd candles Long Will had seen in the windows and narrow slits of the Tor now appeared outside every chamber, even ours some twenty feet above the moat's muddy surface.

In the chapel, where Long Will had gone first to gain some spiritual reinforcement, a friar dressed in a black habit had been seen strolling a foot above the floor and through the baptismal font. He vanished when challenged by Ekaterina's chaplain.

A man in gray garb better suited to the court of Elizabeth than that of Victoria was seen walking across the purely decorative drawbridge over the moat. When he met a tall figure with grim features in a dark cloak pushing a handcart, the guard on the wall above fired his pistol into the air, since neither figure responded to the verbal challenge he issued, and both figures vanished as suddenly as they had appeared.

Sir Rodney had wandered to the chamber door during this dissertation and came back telling us of a faint orange glow seen the corridor, but that no smoke was smelled nor flames seen by him.

At that instance, a bedraggled and damp party of sailors came rushing past our door babbling amongst themselves. We followed, half expecting them to vanish at any moment as they headed towards the duke's chambers. They burst into the room unannounced and awoke the duke at once. To his credit, he was alert as soon as his eyes opened, and his calmness worked like a tonic on our group's frayed nerves.

The appointed speaker, an old-timer named Johansen, told a tall-tale of their small keelboat being swamped by a huge wooden ship of the line built like a galleon. It was heading upstream towards the Kassel and was making excellent time given that there was no wind at all and it lacked a motor to fight the hard current. The only useful details they could recall were a tarnished brass nameplate reading "Marie Deering" and cries of what could have been Dutch or Danish coming from the vessel.

At that, Long Will and I exchanged knowing glances, recalling an odd event we had shared with my late younger brother while en route to Khartoum on board the Bacchante when we, too, had seen an old sailing ship fighting strong currents and contrary winds that appeared and vanished with no warning. At this report, and before I could deliver ours...

Note: Here the hand-written manuscript ends, but the following letter follows on the same leaf in a different hand and in ink.

19 January 1901 AD

To Her Majesty Victoria Regina
At Osborne
From Milton Renfeld,
Keeper of the Braxton Asylum

Your Majesty—

This manuscript was discovered in the chamber lately occupied by your late grandson Albert Victor.

The name written here was struck through, and the phrase "Duke of Clarence" was written in.

Due to the manner of his decease and the possible confidential nature of the writings herein, I decided to send it to you directly. The Prince of Wales has shown no interest in the duke's care since he came to stay with us in the late 1880s, as you well know. I can only imagine what the prince's father would say. Neither my staff nor I have read the document, except for a momentary glance at the handwriting to verify the identity of the author. I await your reply and further instructions via our usual messenger. And I thank you again for the use of a dispatch box for our correspondence.

I remain, your ever loyal and faithful subject—
Milton Renfeld

Ferryman, Don't Tarry

MY FIRST REACTION WHEN THE OLD MAN IN THE THREADBARE LONG, BLACK coat stepped out from behind the huge water oak just below the rip-rap at the old two-lane bridge was to reach for my phone to call the cops to report a homeless man living under the interstate. My second was to stare when he pulled out a long clay pipe and asked for a light and to inwardly roll my eyes about these crazy re-enactors. My third was stunned silence when he spoke…

I have always run the ferry across the Melungeon River just above Dogskull Shoals between Cheslea Falls and Hemphill, even before the towns were more than a house apiece. Ferries have been in my blood as far back as I can remember. The Kephissos, the Tiber, the Mersey, the Thames, the Shannon, the Seine…all have had ferries run by men in my family. Of course, Theseus, the old nigra I bought from old Congressman McGlennan when he ran for Governor back in '38 and lost, helped some, well as much as one of them could. I still ain't sure why he wasted all that time and money and whiskey. Heck, he died the next summer of diphtheria. Caught it from his niece, if my memory serves. And yes, I toted the body from the Hemphill side to the other for the burial out at the meeting house.

At any rate, my first paying customers were the traders going back and forth to swap with the Indians up in the high country and over on the Cheslea bank there. At a silver cent a head and tuppence for a horse and a shilling per wagon or cart, I was doing just dandy. Then, the Scots over in Ireland got to be outnumbered by the Papists and realized that Cromwell was gone, so they had to either go back to the waiting arms of their Jacobite cousins or come over the ocean to seek their fortune. So, they started coming like lemmings to a cliff face. Got Royal grants hand over fist.

Now, since not one in a hundred was Church of England, none of them stayed on the coast in the settlements. Nope, they all came to the back of beyond with folks like us. They all cleared their plots, planted feed from them and the livestock, and built meeting houses. Now, a goodly chunk of the corn would end up in jugs, but I still took it instead of cash money. Heck, chickens and corn liquor may not click and clank in a purse, but they fill a belly. And hell, no one else had any cash and nowhere to spend it if they found any.

Now, even with all this open land, these folks felt constricted by their Indian neighbors, and since they had cleared off the trees to plant, they figgered they'd just go ahead and clear off the Indians, too. And the Cherokee and the Catawba and all decided to push back and, well, lo and behold, the Scots had shoved 'em clean over the mountains.

Now, old Parson Gowiggin tried his damnedest to get the white folk to treat the Indians right, but as long as the Indians kept selling for nothing, the Macs kept on a-buying until the Indians all left. Now, since the good Parson wasn't a Covenanter like most of the Macs, they barely paid him any mind at all until the circuit court judges came through to hear cases over in Hemphill. Then, he dipped, dunked, and married enough folks to keep his body and soul together. Now, he was so cheap and poor he'd try to swim his horse over in all weathers, but he always made his missus use me. Now, since she was a right willing wench at least ten years younger than the Parson, I didn't mind a whit. Not to mention the fact that her cunny was sweeter than honeydew vine water and just as wet. I was always glad to give her a lift and a ride in lieu of hard cash. He never caught on as far as I know and thanked the Lord for his children whether he helped make them in his image or not.

After the Indians got pushed back, things began to heat up among the Macs and the folks down in Charleston. Folks hereabouts kept kicking for judges to come and to be left alone by the Parson, and the folks in Charleston didn't pay them no nevermind until the English decided to make the colonists start helping pay their way with new taxes. Then everybody started getting along fine, since none of them wanted to pay taxes or board the Kings Own anyway.

So, of course, a new war started up in New England. Folks down this way mainly used it as an excuse to settle old scores while the bigwigs bickered about who exactly was in charge. Then, Old Cornwallis came down and made folks pick sides for serious. I toted soldiers and horses and cannons across and back on this river 'til I thought I'd flat out die. I didn't care two whits about who won this battle or that, as long as the money was good. Heck, I toted Generals Davie and Davidson over before Davidson got kilt up above Charlotte after I toted old General Gates across after he got whupped like a rented mule in Camden. I always wondered how he got so far ahead of his troops, but I figgered he just had a better horse.

A while later, I toted Colonel Tarleton and his fellas over, but he stiffed me on the fare. Naturally, I was tickled to hear that Ole Dan Morgan and Billy Washington beat his arse at Hannah's Cowpens just after.

So, of course, I made it through the war just fine. Hell, I was able to claim some bounty land for all the cash fares that never got paid. Got a hundred acres on the far side of the river and another five hundred over in Kentucky or somewheres. Built me a sizable farm over on the small piece and sold the big one for better than a dollar an acre to some general. At least *he* paid in gold. Spanish money, too, which spends just like the rest.

Now, with having a bigger place, I had to have some slaves. I bought a few from neighbors, but I had to get about a dozen brand new ones just off the boat for some breed stock. Well, that was just damn sad. I bought two whole families and three or four buckras and you never heard the like. From Charleston all the way up past Granby they cried and chanted and wept. I had one try to sneak off just below Camden, but when I grabbed its babe by the ankles and made a move to bash it against a tree, he came slinking back and never gave me no more real trouble.

I raised enough food to stay alive, enough corn to make likker to sell for extry money, and enough cotton to make me mad, but my heart was on the river.

Now, I never was much for politics, but we always have had some humdingers in these parts. Johnny Calhoun and his friends were changeable, but they did well by us for a long time. Shoot, they got the canal built just above us here. Now, they couldn't find no boats to use it, but I don't blame them for that none.

Now, I was a fan of General Andy Jackson from the day he got slapped by the British officer with his sword for back-sassing. It helped that I knew his daddy before he got sick, too. So when John Calhoun fell out with the general over some floozy, I backed Andy all the way. Which some folks hereabouts took wrong, but they got over it quick when I told 'em that I didn't cotton to no bad talk about my fella and that I'd put the boat up and just let 'em all sit on the bank 'til the second coming before I'd fight over it. Hell, it beat having to fight a duel a day to prove that the man was right when I didn't have a dog in that fight.

Besides that mess, the only real excitement I had was when I toted a fugitive slave across the river and damned near got hung for it. It was about the time we picked that spat with Santa Ana over Californy. Now, he had a signed pass to go across the river to deliver some medicine to the Widow Ponds over near Hemphill, not to mention the dime for the fare, so I carried him across.

Imagine my dismay when about twenty fellows on horseback with long arms came up with as many baying hounds. They threw me against the side of the boat and demanded to know why I took Hadrian across the river. I fought back my natural inclination to reply that Hadrian had been dead for over a thousand years and simply told them that he had a pass signed by Old Man McCalla to take some tonic to the widow.

The spokesman and Hadrian's erstwhile overseer, a hothead named Jackie Donovan, called me a liar and offered to stretch my neck to help me recall the truth. I denied his claim and told them to ask the widow since I had seen the tonic and it was broad daylight. After some whispered consultation and some sips of the handiest jug, Donovan called me a liar again and told me that Hadrian had forged his daddy's signature on the pass after Donovan had sold Hadrian's missus and their kids down the river to a place over in Arkansas.

Well, at that, my sympathy went wholly to the poor black bastard and repeated my claim of innocence again. I told Donovan to change his way of doing passes, since his nigras could out-sign his pappy, and the party stormed off downstream.

A few months later, young Master Donovan met with a tragic accident while out hunting deer. His horse reared suddenly after encountering a rattler on the riverbank and threw him into the water, which was high after three weeks of steady rain. He drowned and his battered body was found about three miles downstream. No one noticed the bullet hole at the base of his neck with all the other cuts and bruises inflicted by the debris in the torrent.

After the excitement caused by Hadrian's escapade died down, things quickly returned to normal. I'd tote a few traders across the river during the day, then a large number of churchgoers on Sunday. The rates didn't change either. A dime a head and a quarter per buggy, wagon or coach, and tuppence a barrel or bushel for freight, and most folks managed to pay cash, though I still took barter if I had to—or if the gal was young, pretty, and ready to swap her innocence for my pleasure.

The politicians made their usual racket about slavery and territory and such, but I didn't pay no nevermind. Not 'til that black Republican ape Lincoln got elected and everything started hopping like water in a skillet.

First, the South seceded and started raising an army. Then they started bragging about how quick they'd whup the Yankees and all. Of course, they tried to draft me to volunteer, but I had to run the ferry because damned if I'd let Theseus try to run it by himself.

But I made a booming business of toting the flower of Hemphill County's youth over the river so they could catch the train to Charlotte or Columbia from Cheslea Falls. And for the first year or two of the war, I'd get repaid in Confederate money that was worth something by the state. Those boys were a hoot. Half of them had never fired a gun in anger, and the rest had only shot at squirrels, partridge, and the occasional doe. None of them could imagine what army life was going to be like, and they didn't care to learn. Of course, better than half the ones who came home were missing pieces, and half all the ones that went stayed under strange soil and never again saw the South Carolina sun. All for some half-baked dream of some politician and a racist grudge, such a damned waste, but the coffin carvers and the gravediggers made a mint.

By the end of the war, after Sherman went through Georgia like a rich sailor at a whorehouse, the spirits of the boys being sent north to fight were lower than a hound's tail after a scalding. Folks around here lost their damned minds. Tried to wreck Jeff Davis's getaway train and steal the Confederate Treasury. Of course, they also thought Sherman himself was coming to burn everything bigger than a breadbox.

Well, I got stuck dodging the Conscription men, who mainly wanted to milk me for a bounty payment to keep my exemption and running this ole boat. I carried the last batch to go try to slow up Grant in Virginia just afore Lee gave up the ghost, then danged if I didn't carry supplies for one of old Sherman's Corps right after. The fellows were real closed-mouthed about their boss, but it's hard to hide a Boston Yankee accent, especially when I know every living soul within a twenty mile radius. But their money was made of gold, not paper worth less than a re-used corncob in a privy, so I kept their secret and played my part of dumb hick.

Well, it wasn't long after that than most of my traffic was Yankee troops in uniform, tight-mouthed old biddies with Yankee accents, and beady-eyed chaps with frizzy beards and tiny little pince-nezs. Dang near every one of them was coming west from up in Charlotte and Raleigh to educate our nigras and train us to be good little Christian Republicans, since dang near every inch of railroad track from Baltimore to New Orleans was gone. I had to tote just about all of them, whether they stayed in Hemphill or not.

Most of the beady-eyed types admitted they were here to get rich and go home, which made me roar since every field within sight was burnt black, there wasn't a United States penny to be had for miles about and the Confederate money was as much good as a newspaper from eighteen and twenty. All those abolitionist women were real tight with both their money and their favors unless you were a new-freed slave man, which made both us white fellas and the black ladies real upset with them. Not that I'd ask for the favors. With so many young men either dead or crippled, my dance card stayed full, even with my advanced age and odd ways.

Now, the same thing that gave me so much companionship led to a whole big chuck of folks going belly-up completely. For at least two years after the war, getting crops planted and harvested was a second or third thought at best. So a lot of folks never paid their taxes on the land. Those beady-eyed fellas I mentioned before managed to pay the back taxes and got a hold of a sizable piece of the county. At least 'til the Ku Kluxers got organized and loaded for bear. Then the abolitionist beauties started finding partners for afternoon delights in the old schoolhouse kind of scarce. And, for some reason, a ton of those beady-eyed fellas got to be fond of rope swings and impromptu swimming parties in the dead of night.

In fact, about a half mile downstream, there's a spot called the boiler hole that quite a few found to be to their liking. I reckon swimming lessons aren't a big part of the schooling up north because most of the ones that went down there stayed. And I will concede that it's harder to swim in a hemp necklace and boots. Course, all those type antics simply made the politicians in Washington mad and led to more Yankee troops coming to eat us out of house and home. They stayed 'til old Wade Hampton cleaned out Columbia of… As suddenly as the odd old man had appeared he was gone, right in mid-sentence.

The roar of the traffic from the bridge on the interstate highway over the Melungeon grew louder and drowned out the end of his sentence. I was still standing there in shock alone when my rod man and my assistant joined me to see which way the sewer line we were surveying needed to run. They thought I had either seen or been bitten by a water moccasin. They were too far away to hear any of the conversation, and the ground cover obscured their sightline. All they knew was that I was non-responsive to repeated calls over the walkie-talkies and standing stock still at the end of our cut line near the bridge.

Having heard that the woods near the highway bridge were haunted, neither of them wanted to be caught there at twilight, which was closing fast. My rod man made the command decision to move the work truck around to the bridge to pick me and the equipment up and left my assistant, who was on his first assignment with us out of the office, to gather me up the rip-rap and bank next to the interstate.

As we walked, I asked over and over what time the ferry would be in. Neither my rod man nor my assistant would answer me. Finally, when we stopped to gas up, and I seemed to be more myself, I went inside to get a drink and happened to ask the girl behind the counter the same question. Her reaction was to slap me silly, call the cops, and smile when I was taken to the hospital. They treated me for exhaustion, but I know what my real problem was.

I'm overdue to catch my ferry, and I can't find anyone who can make change for oboloi out of a dollar. I'm in need of a rest and simply must have my fare. I can't wander on the riverbank.

ALL SOULS, ALL SAINTS

ON THE NIGHT OF NOVEMBER SECOND, THE SOULS OF THOSE WHO HAVE DIED over the past year gather at a crossroads in the foothills of the Carolinas. Stories whispered in the darkest corners of dives and dumps throughout the region mention the possibility of awesome power being loosed to be gained by the bold or foolhardy. Of course, these same tales mention the after-effects of intruding on the communion of the dead, even the faithful departed. Drifters were serving multiple life sentences for crimes too horrible to contemplate that they were innocent of, for the dead are as jealous of their privacy as the living but have more ways to ensure it. But even with the terrors lurking, folks couldn't and wouldn't leave well enough alone for whatever reason. Because whispers born in buck-a-cup diners just before daylight bear strange fruit in honkey-tonks just before closing time. Old men thought stupid by neighbors serve as oracles, dredging up the bones of the forgotten past from the riverbed of memory just half-dimmed by a lifetime of labor and liquor. Unreceptive college kids serve as willing antennae, picking up pieces of folklore and building puzzles to bewitch and befuddle those pressing from behind. The smoke-stained cinderblock walls and scuffed hardwood floors amplify the past into a near-living presence, hanging on the listeners gathered like the notes of the done wrong song blaring from the battered jukebox. The tales told by Hanks and Georges and Johnnys cannot compete with the mysteries revealed at the corner stool.

I heard about the gathering when I was in high school from a fifth-year senior while we shared a jug of homemade peach brandy and a joint from my personal patch. He said that just after dark on the night of the second, the dead appeared in hooded white robes like monks and formed circles in the road around a central point that was empty. He reckoned that the circles must be formed by denomination. Since Methodists didn't speak to Baptists at the liquor store on Earth, why would the other world be any different? After all the dead arrived and formed their ranks, the circles began to converge toward the center. As each circle was drawn to a point, a flicker of flame and loud bang marked their departure for their eternal reward. He blithely answered all my questions, like could you tell who was who and did they look like they did when they had all died or like they were in new bodies like the preacher said and why do we still got ghosts? Now, I was concerned because my uncle Ricky had passed about three months before and the cancer had whupped his ass and changed him from being a big fun-loving fella to a scrawny, crybaby of a wuss. In fact, the only question he couldn't or wouldn't BS his way through was where the hell all this happened. When I asked that, he clammed up like I had said I was a narc and was there to lock him up. Hell, the sumbitch walked off and kept my damn lighter... and the roach, too.

Now, I wrote the whole conversation off as the babbling of a terminal "show-out" until I starting dating a good Catholic girl in college. She drug me to Mass on November the second, which was a Tuesday of all days, instead of her place for our usual romp and looked at me like I was the slowest kid in class when I asked what the occasion was. With an eye roll, she set me straight. It was a Requiem Mass in honor of the recently departed, hence All Souls Day. The memory of that long-ago chat came back to me and, for a change, I paid attention to the ceremony, hopeful of gleaning some more information. I even caught the priest after the service and asked if he knew anything about the gathering and got a stink-eye back in return. I didn't think priests could do that, but now you know. Well, for whatever reason, this made me decide to hunt down this gathering. One good thing about the college I went to was the sheer number of different folks running around. You could find somebody from some off-beat place or somebody who believed in strange shit with ease. Hell, if you hit three different bars within three blocks of campus, you'd fall into the arms of the local ACT UP chapter, the faculty bitch-fest and booze-up, or the La Raza outfit offering how-to classes on Santeria. Well, I decided to wear out the library first, like a good nerd with a new fixation after getting stonewalled by both my History of Southern Culture professor and the chair of the religion department.

Blackwood College was blessed by virtue of it being the oldest private college north of Charleston. Folks had been giving papers and letters to the archives since it was founded, and the archivist, Herbert Gebel, was deaf as a post and as wide as he was tall, all six foot of it. I swear had been there since the dedication, but he knew his stuff. When I mentioned I was interested in legends from the area on All Souls Day, he nodded and wandered off into the stacks. Before I could pull out my laptop and notebook, he was back with four big gray boxes overflowing with papers and a cart full of leather-bound ledger-sized tomes. He mumbled something about WPA and Mansards and Margaret Murray and cleared ground in high places and walked off back to his desk. Well, ninety percent of the stuff in the boxes was just illegible. I mean, buckras, hants and mebbe, and all that stuff. But I managed to sift out enough stuff to decide that the story might have something to it. It was just snatches and pieces pulled out from between the lines, but I knew that over towards the Blue Ridge Escarpment near Lake Sataree, there were several likely spots due to the terrain and the tales I had found. Looking Glass Cliffs right on the state line was the likely culprit if the roads matched.

So I decided to round up some buddies for a combination road trip and hike. Sadly, by this point, me and Kate had broken up. I wasn't ready for confirmation, and she wasn't ready to be fashionably agnostic yet, so we wandered apart except for the occasional, and later regretted, booty call after or during a bender. I called my buddy Bobby, who everybody called Chick after he ate two twenty-piece buckets of gas-station chicken on a bet and lived, and convinced him that the best way to spend the weekend after a Halloween drunk was out in the woods. Thankfully the Lord do look out for fools and little children, and I ain't in need of no diaper change. After several issues with folks wanting to vote while in possession of their hunting rifles, both state legislatures decided to push the start of deer season back to the Saturday after Election Day. So we wouldn't have to dodge any physical bullets, and since the state was trying to locate a state park at Looking Glass Cliffs and that side of Santaree, we wouldn't be trespassing on the living at any case.

According to the map I had sketched based on the old letters I had found in the archives, two old logging roads crossed about a quarter mile back of the cliff face at Looking Glass. One of the old roads had started life as an Indian trading path between the Cherokees and the Catawbas, and the other was meant to be the Charleston to Charleston Turnpike that was never built all the way through. The spot would be hard to miss even with the mountain top having been clear-cut in the last decade or so since a small family cemetery was located right at the old intersection. We were able to drive all the way up to the edge of the tree line before the ruts got too bad for my sports car to handle. Hey, I was in college...practical wasn't a priority by a far piece. We piled out and shouldered our packs for the miles and miles of hard hiking looming before us. Um, no. We walked maybe five hundred feet to the middle of the clearing. Old Chick just about got re-circumcised by the spiked post of the wrought iron fence around a busted-up table tomb. I told him to lay off the beer, but he just burped in my general direction. We found a likely spot between the old intersection and the car and pitched our tents. Now, me and Chick had been friends for years, but we weren't about to sleep together. After we got all that straight, we gathered up deadfall for a campfire and grabbed enough big rocks to set up a fire-ring big enough to suit. We weren't out to melt beer cans, but neither one of us wanted to freeze either. The Carolina foothills in November ain't exactly Phoenix in August, especially after dark. After we had a fire worthy of the name, we headed back to the car and grabbed some hot dogs and beer out of the cooler and made supper. Now we only brought two cases of beer since it was just the two of us and we were only out for the night, so you'll forgive us for not sitting up 'til midnight chatting about love, life, and where the bodies are buried. Me and Chick each grabbed the beers we had left, our Walkmans, and sacked out. We both agreed we'd wake the other one when the show started up. I knew I'd be up after slamming back beer like it was water in the desert. I found the Gamecocks game on the radio. The Vols were beating them stupid, so I gave up on them at the half and popped in a mix tape of weird junk I'd found messing around in a buddy's LP collection. Well, about half way through Bob Willis doing "Pan Handle Rag," I must have dozed off since I awoke to a terrifying sight. Chick was staring down at me shirtless whispering my name over and over. After shoving him out the open tent flap, I sat up and grunted. As I grabbed my boots and realized that my bladder had been swapped out for the Atlantic Ocean, I caught a glimpse of a faint glimmer of white light from over Chick's pasty shoulder.

"That's why I woke you up. That and your snoring were giving every bear between here and Asheville a boner. It's right at quarter 'til midnight. The light show just started. Be real careful when you wander off to piss. It's as black as Bonnie's heart out there otherwise. Moon must be back of a cloud or something. And to top it all off, the damn ground is froze. I bumped against the side of my tent coming over here, and it sounded like I dropped a box of beer mugs."

Using my usual stunning wit, I told Chick to try to crap out his own head and headed for the tree line to pee. Well, I thought it was the tree line at least. Instead I got a mite bewildered in the pitch black, which shocked me because usually there is some light bleeding over from Greenville and Spartanburg, and headed to the cliff face. I peed with no trouble until I turned to come back. I slipped on a rock and was bound on the express to Santaree. Thankfully most of the beer I'd had was gone, and I managed to grab a tree root and holler for Chick. Of course it came out in a whisper, but the big lummox heard it and came over to haul me up. He only banged me on three rocks and didn't manage to break my rubber band of a shoulder.

"Damn boy, you can't fly. Now, you alright enough to run a Polaroid?"

I was amazed Chick had the presence of mind to remember the camera. Our plan was to get enough pictures to prove the arrival of the recently departed and sell to whichever tabloid would pay off our student loans. We were going to get shots of the area during the gathering and in the morning. I had brought a blank tape to stick in the Walkman just in case it might help. I threw a quick glance over to the intersection and noticed the light was a bit brighter. I nodded at Chick and whispered that I needed to grab the tape from the car and we'd start up.

Right about the time I got back, things started to come to a rolling boil. Chick was already taking shots as the first ring of the dead formed. The flash from the Polaroid was as feeble as a thimble emptying Lake Santaree and was soon as useless. The circles were as dense as growth rings on a chunk of redwood in a museum when I heard Chick grumble a "damn" as the first sleeve of shots ran out. I stole a glance at the tape in the Walkman and noticed that it had not budged. I pressed the rewind button to make sure the thing wasn't dead when I felt eyes on me.

I slowly turned and locked eyes with Tony Burris, the same pothead who'd told me about this event all those years ago. No flicker of recognition animated his features at first. Then he smirked and brought his chin to his chest. I hadn't spoken to Tony since that night in the peach orchard, and as he looked away, a sudden memory popped up like an ad on the internet. That morning at breakfast I had glanced through the local paper and had scanned the obits. Tony was in there, but it hadn't rung a bell at the time. Hell, no college kid reads the obits, so sue me. About the same instant I had recalled and dismissed the memory, I was stunned to find me and Tony face-to-face, and he spoke.

"You are fortunate tonight. Had I not been called home by my own foolish actions last night, you would be in great peril. Your friend will be among us next year, and you will bear the guilt for it, if not the actual blame, unless he too has someone to intercede. I did not tell you of this for you to pry untimely. I thought the tale was one told by old wives myself and would serve to impress the less experienced until now. Too many just shrug, but the foolhardy have blazed the trail for you and added to our numbers. Rashness is not the aftereffects of poison ivy."

At this point, a sudden movement in the corner of my eye diverted my attention back to Chick to my own dismay. He was surrounded by figures bearing the causes of their coming in Technicolor gore. Livid red scars and gashes seemed to glow in the brightening glare, which was unaffected by the thickening haze and mist on the margins of the masses. I watched the half dozen encircling Chick pantomime the acts that had brought them hence and watched the color drain from his face like watching suds from a busted washing machine. I heard Tony's voice in my head and turned back to where he… stood? Hovered? Waited? What word works for a spirit telling you that a friend may well die tonight and that it was your fault? At any rate, he resumed his discussion like I had not interrupted or impeded his thoughts in the least.

"Like all those who have before you, you seek, but not for right reasons. You seek for glory… for gold… for fame. Knowledge should be sought for the knowing. The knowing is what raises us above the mere animal. Even they seek, but you notice they also respect."

With a start, it came to me that we had heard no bird calls nor even seen so much as a crow's feather the entire day. Heck, I had jokingly mentioned we might eat venison based on the fact my last trip up this way was marked by the sighting of six deer in an afternoon and part of an evening. We hadn't even seen the flicker of a whitetail.

"They know this night is sacred and stay away. 'Tis a shame even the basest of beasts have more sense than some men. This is why your friend will suffer for your folly. He came as a mere parasite, with no more interest than the bookworm has for the content of the page it feasts upon."

Hoping that the recently dead worked on the same theory as a Bond villain, I decided to find some gumption and keep Tony talking. I prayed that I could figure out a way for us to avoid what seemed to be our iron-clad doom as he did. Of course, I had no idea what we'd discuss. Somehow, football, girls, and fast cars didn't seem to appeal at the moment. I decided to try to find out what exactly Chick did to deserve whatever was coming down the fast lane.

"Dude, we were buds of a sort. What did he ever do to you? I'm the one who drug him up here. Why not make me suffer?"

"Ah, me. You have been told why. He came as an...appendage. A mere tool even. Hold a camera and try to make money off something he will never understand. No, he will suffer for your folly and his. Our sled needs grease for the runners as it were. You are actually fortunate not to share his fate. As I said, had I not been called last night, you both would bear our wounds."

I noticed with some degree of alarm that the light had begun to dim. A stolen peek at my watch told me that it was about five 'til midnight. Something in my gut told me that time was running out quicker than cops to a donut shop on free coffee day. I'm a smart guy, so maybe if I deciphered what the hell was up, I could still get us off the hook before the big fish swallowed us both.

"Okay, but listen before you dig in, so to speak. What exactly is going on? Where's the light coming from, and why is it fading out? What do you mean, bear our wounds? Like stigmata or what?"

"Very simple. He will bear our literal wounds. Every cut, every bullet hole, every broken bone. Every aliment. Every burnt-up chemo port and every collapsed fistula. Stigmata are for the saintly, not the stupidly. You will pass as an audience and pay the corporeal price for both your sins. A fair enough trade to my mind. Now, time drains to the last grains..."

The light was just about gone. The wispy yet strangely solid figures surrounding Chick pressed closer. I swear at least two were inside his clothes with him. He hadn't uttered so much as a squeak since Tony started talking, which for Chick meant that he was asleep, dead, or that I had gone deaf. Chick seemed to still be breathing, though he was scared shitless and paler than the White House in a blizzard. I gave him an unnoticed wink and started back up with Tony.

"Whoa a minute. I'm still all eat up with questions. Why here? Surely Sassafras or even Table Rock offer more...appropriate places for such a momentous event. Why Looking Glass Cliffs? I haven't heard of any great religious outpourings in these parts. Heck, even the Cherokee ignored this garden spot."

Tony nodded, I reckoned in agreement, and began to hold forth again. For a guy who couldn't pass PE in high school, being dead made him both a bore and a genius.

"Ah, the folly of youth and the ignorance of a true provincial. You don't even know what you don't know. The modern has obscured the truth. Here, let me remove the set dressing of today and show you the essence of this place."

With that, he poked me in the forehead with his index finger in the universal gesture for "think." Immediately after, my head swam, and after my vision cleared, Tony and I were alone on the cliff face looking toward Asheville. Lake Santaree was gone and so was any aspect of civilization. Instead, I saw two prominent ridges flanked and divided by three rivers, all falling off to the north. With a shrug, I looked over at Tony. The utter absence of Chick, his tormentors, and the ambient glow of the recently departed registered like a beer fart at a water treatment plant, if at all.

"You are seeing the Chegree Falls basin. Chegree is Cherokee for 'the two-backed beast,' a giant with the face of a turkey buzzard, a split upper body of a beautiful maiden on the left side but a hunchbacked old man on the right and the legs and feet of a bear with the addition of the tail of a skink, which it used to flail its victims tender and reattached after. What you call Looking Glass Cliffs is better known as Chegreeloos, its lair and feasting place. Chegree served the Cherokee as a way to cleanse the Earth of evil men and their remains. Tribe members guilty of the basest behavior and egregious taboo breaking were brought here and offered two choices…walk off or get thrown off. Those who walked were offered some hope of redemption after several painful cycles of reincarnation, after passing through the digestive system of the beast a few times for purification. Those who had to have…help served as object lessons and bogie-men for bad children after fertilizing the river bottom below. The spot we now stand on was one of the most sacred spots in the region and was highly taboo. Only reigning chiefs and high holy men were allowed here when not performing ceremonial tasks. This system worked for over a millennium until the Cherokee were defeated in the 1770 War. The Mansard family won Chegreeloos as part of a massive land grant for their role in avenging the massacre of the Hamptons. The spot was left in its usual natural state until the Reverend Laurens Hayne bought the mountain and another three hundred acres to serve as base for a prospective colony of freed mixed-race slaves after the Revolution to be known as Moultriesborough. Sadly, the good Reverend was a better promoter than planner. Only twenty of the expected two hundred colonists came up from Charleston, and the local squatters took offense at the arrival of them to boot. The Reverend did build a house and a small church, leading to the clearing we now occupy. However, he could not adjust to the cold weather after being born and bred in Barbados and died right after the church was finished. His heir was a bit…peculiar at least. Unlike most of his white brethren, he decided that the natives knew better how to cope with the realities of mountain living. Now he did keep the Lord in his proper place, but no self-respecting Christian would have recognized his doctrine. Chegree returned from obscurity and served to punish sinners far quicker than He could. The only problem was that the Mansards kept the small cemetery plot your friend stumbled across and interrupted the punishment of McBee Mansard's mistress for fornication during the funeral of McBee's eldest boy, Pinckney. Of course, the mourners, who were all armed in spite of their solemn duty, wiped out the handful of cultists. After the internment, they returned and put the shacks of the colonists to the torch and sold the colonists down the river to Alabama and other points southwest. Following in the footsteps of the Romans, they went as far as to actually sow salt in the earth, which is why this spot is so barren even now. You know the Mansards wound up moving to Texas and are now largely forgotten hereabouts except for the name of the dam at Santaree. Hence the fact that the spot has been 'ignored' all these years. By the time the WPA braved the moonshiners and bad roads to investigate the area's folklore and folkways, the Mansards were as gone as the colonists and Chegree."

"Okay, but why would the recently departed be gathering here? I'm sure more folks died on Earth in the last year than the handful I've seen here. Where are the rest? Is that the Light?"

When I spoke, the vista returned to the present. The ridges and rivers were gone, re-absorbed into the calm waters of Santaree. I stole a peek at my watch in the still dimmer glow and saw it was about two 'til midnight. I hoped Tony wasn't done showing off his new-found smarts quite yet, but I still had no idea what I was going to do to get Chick and me out of this damned mess.

"Every continent has its own spot, and all of them have ties to traditions far older than the Christian, though all have been used by the Son for His own ends. Oh, my yes, many more gathered last night over on Brown Mountain. The Light comes from Heaven and serves to winnow us, like in the parable of the Sheep and the Goats. Those who have fallen short of immediate arrival in Bliss gather here to be sorted further. The Light has gathered those who died of no fault but nature's. Disease and age, mingle with the prayers of loved ones to bring them to Glory a beat behind those who died blameless in toto and forgiven. The dimming of the Light means that almost all have been called home to the Father. Those of us who remain need to slough off our marks and make our final dispensation. Not all who are called go to the Father. The Devil does get his due, until the trump sounds at least. My intercession on your behalf may send me to Limbo in lieu of another place, if He so chooses. Now, the time for idle talk is at an end."

"Whoa, whoa, whoa. Hold on a second. Who gathered at Brown Mountain? What was the deal with last night? I thought all the dead were here now."

"No, you fool. The Saints, those who died in a state of forgiveness and in communion with the Father gathered on Brown Mountain last night. The lights are seen year-round as souls trickle in, but the Rosa only forms once a year. At midnight on the first of November, the Saints who passed in the preceding year gather en masse just above the summit and form the Mystic Rose. *That* is what you should have sought, but like all mortals, the Spina has more attractive for the danger and excitement it offers."

"What the heck is the Spina? I'm here because of that wild tale you told back in school. Chick is only here as a solid to me. This whole danged mess is *your* fault. Mystic Roses? Really? Sheep and goats? What is all this, Sunday School?"

"No, all happens for a reason, my friend. Had I not been called yesterday and not been here tonight, you both would pay for your trespass. The reason your friend will be gifted with our marks is simple. The body will be reborn, but only after the dross is burnt off or given to another. We will be perfect on Judgment Day, but a scapegoat must be found to bear our scars and sins. Your friend speeds that plow for us and ensures he will sit at the feet of the Throne on that day for his service. Look upon him. The ecstasy he now feels will and has trumped the agony. He will be first on Brown Mountain next year and see the Father that much the sooner. The old song was more right than the author knew. Every Rose has its Thorn. Now, no more idle chat."

With that, I was left alone, on the margin of what followed. I stood at the tree line with my heart in my throat and a scream on my lips. Chick looked my way once, and I made a move his way, but he waved me off. As I watched, he convulsed once and was stripped to the skin and every bone in his body was damn near ground to powder. I stared aghast, locked in place as surely as if I were in a cage while every wound imaginable suddenly appeared on the boy. The truly bizarre part was that his expression never changed from a grin that in other circumstances would be called dopey. His eyes rolled back in his head, and he was gently laid on the very edge of the cliff. He still breathed and looked to be alive. As the last glimmer of the glow faded and the usual night sounds returned after an honestly unnoticed absence, I broke and ran to him. I reached his side and began to do CPR because what else could I do? When I started doing the chest compressions, his eyes opened, and he screamed. I looked up and saw a pair of eyes completely devoid of life or light look back into mine from the empty air, completely obscuring the vista of the lake and the twinkling lights on its distant shores. The eyes were bad enough, but the jet black and gore-splattered beak bigger than I was made me retch and jump back like a crab fleeing a flashlight. When I landed on my butt, the beak engulfed Chick, and eyes and beak both vanished below my line of sight. I lunged forward and caught a glimpse of two reddish-tan backs as broad as a doublewide trailer heading for the lake. Then I felt a smack on the side of my head and went ass over tea kettle over the rock face.

Whoever said booty calls were a bad thing never met Kate. I had called her on Halloween night after a vodka-fueled night of ghost hunting and random riding. At some point in the five-minute message I left from a pay phone in Five Points, I mentioned that me and Chick were off to see the "Gathering of the Recently Departed" over at Looking Glass Cliffs and did she want tag along for some loving under the stars. Well, when I didn't answer her call back or call her back at all, she got worried and drove up on that Sunday afternoon after Mass.

Thankfully, neither Chick nor I followed the whole "leave no trace" concept on that trip. She drove right to the car, hollered for us both, and packed all our crap up and put it all in my car. Then she said she heard a moan from the cliff, peeked over the edge despite being horrified of heights, and saw me on a ledge about two hundred feet down. Thanks to her folks and money and being paranoid, she had a car phone and even had service way out in the sticks. She called in EMS and the Med-Evac copter to pick me up. I was alive (duh) but had broken both arms just above the wrists and had cut my face up good on my way down. The medics were amazed that I didn't break my fool neck. I spent the night in the hospital getting fluids and generally getting worked over. Stitches across the sternum and both knees hurt by the way and itched like hell. Kate was a pre-med major and was interning as an ER nurse, so I was told that I'd be staying with her until I got better.

She didn't listen to the weak argument I gave to stay by myself and told her brother to pack up my dorm room and bring it to her apartment. Her brother and I had played American Legion baseball together before our freshman year at Blackwood, and he was about six-four and two-fifty of pure Irish Catholic muscle. I was in no shape to argue, and if I had tried to or was in shape to, he would have folded me up, put me in his backpack, and did what she said anyway.

Well, I got back in one piece after a few weeks. Kate said she never found Chick but that some hunters found his clothes about a mile from the car in the woods. She said that the cops thought that some wild animal had attacked us in the night and carried off Chick and I freaked out and ran over the cliff either half-asleep on in a blind panic.

She asked me what I remembered, and I gave her a highly-sanitized version of the chat with Tony and the attack on Chick. I left out the part about the beak and eyes when she gave a stare normally given to lying children or street prophets. She soothed me during the nightmares, and we got back together. Hell, I even joined the Church, which pleased her folks and made my proposal that much easier to accept. In fact, things have been fine since, except for the black bruise on my forehead I can't get to clear up and the urge I have to head to Brown Mountain every Halloween night.

DEVIL TAKES A DAY

WHEN I'M NOT IN CHARGE OF TORMENTING SOULS AND GENERALLY RUNNING things in Hell, I do enjoy my time off. For Heaven's sake, even I enjoy the wonders of creation. After all, most of them were *my* idea. (Note to self: Hire better writers next time.) God got all the press, and all I got was the music.

I'm a huge fan of the Carolinas for some reason. I reckon the long tradition of general hell-raising and an independence of spirit seem to touch me in some special place. That and the general hypocrisy, of course. Baptists don't speak to Methodists at the Red Dots. Methodists don't speak to Presbyterians at the dance halls. And Episcopalians just cash the checks every Monday. I love it.

And the scenic beauty in some spots does seem to clear my mind of the shrieks of the demons I lord over and the screams of the sinners they torment. Forty Acre Rock, over near Taxahaw, is nice. Has been ever since Tarleton did such good work getting it ready for me during the Revolution. The Devil's Tramping Ground up near Siler City used to be nice, but the local kids have decided to turn it into a drinking spot, which impedes my pacing, even when I do kick them out of the way. But like all proud parents, I do have my favorite, even if it's not quite as famous yet.

The Congaree River bluffs down near Columbia are just lovely, especially in the springtime. I especially like Congaree National Park. Nice and quiet and just far enough off the beaten path that I can run up and do some thinking and not be bothered. Plus, if a few rowdy college kids get drunk and wander off into the swamp, is it *really* my fault every time?

At any rate, you have old-growth forests and black-water swamps. And the occasional pack of "wild dogs" that no one has ever actually seen but that everyone within a five-mile radius has heard in full cry. Poor Swamp Girl, still trying to get home to her sick momma every time a thunder storm pops up in the summer time, which seems to happen every time I visit. At least she's pretty, so she can get rides *almost* to Columbia proper. Or the old coach and four that goes careening down the old logging roads without heed to any obstacles, be they trees, trucks, or even the occasional lost hiker. But my favorite diversion is the Dutchman of the Congaree, because I actually had a little something to do with that one.

Back before the Civil War (I love that name. It was about as civil as a bar fight.), there was a fair amount of barge traffic on the Congaree below Columbia and a good number of ferries crossing it at various low points. One of the busiest was located a little bit downstream from the current National Park and was called Motte's Ferry. Now, every other week a particular barge would be poled up-river with a crew of about a half-dozen slaves and one professional drunkard of a captain. For the life of me, I can't recall his name, but oh well. After an extended drought, the river had gotten a bit lower than usual. This, combined with the very heavy fog on the river, made navigation even more hazardous than usual. This extra stress led the captain to call upon me for assistance.

"I'll swap my soul even up to clear this damnable fog and make up my time!" he shouted into the mist. Taking that as my cue, I appeared before him.

I asked again, to clarify, "What boon do you desire for the trifling price of one's soul? After all, 'tis a dear bargain to make."

"Clear this damned fog and give me good water to the wharf in Columbia, and better wine or begone!" was his heartfelt and sincere reply. His sheer volume of his shout caused much consternation among the horses waiting for the ferry upriver.

"No, sir, that I cannot do for the price you offer. But I am a fair man, despite any rumors you may have heard. I can still be of assistance if you vow to uphold this bargain, freely made," I replied in a quiet voice, knowing it would inspire the fool to purest fury.

"What good is a soul if you can't feed the body? Hush you mewling babes, or I'll lash you to the very marrow! Whatever you will do will be just fine. Just be timely with it!"

"My good man, you have made a very wise choice, *but* your problem is not the level of the water, but the weight of the vessel."

With that, I claimed the flesh and souls of his crew as a mere snack. Then I leaned in close to his ear and whispered, "Now, the boat will make excellent time. I am sorry, but I must take my payment now. Too many defaulters of late."

A few moments later, witnesses reported seeing a flash like an arsenal had exploded, though no noise followed, and then the deserted barge drifted into the bank below the ferry and sank in less than ten feet of water.

Locals claim the barge reappears on the anniversary of the crash, but that anyone foolhardy enough to witness the sinking winds up dead within the next year. All I can say to that is, I need to be going. I have some things to collect.

THE CONFESSION OF CINNEAUS THE LAZARITE

THE DARK MAN CAME ON FOOT AS HE HAD BEEN TOLD. HIS SEA-GREEN ROBE was spotless and glimmered in the midday sun. The sea breeze swirled it around his feet as he crested the hill to the open gate before him. He paused to regain his wind and glanced back over his shoulder. Below him rose the gleaming white marble spire of the Arch Magus's palace. Beyond the stone pile before him and its scattered wooden outbuildings lay the Nordsee. To his left, he heard the shouts of fishermen rising from a hidden harbor. Toria Priory was a squat stone building surrounded by a high stone wall that served more for decoration than protection, though the dark man knew that only a fool or a desperate man would scale it without invitation. A young man of twenty, tanned and in excellent condition, waved at the approaching figure.

The young man led the dark figure through the open mosaicked courtyard down a pathway lined with columns. The man spoke as they passed a large chamber furnished with a large square table and lined with benches built over rows of strongboxes. On the walls hung a large painting of a party of adventurers faced with a peril the dark man could not see. This was flanked by glass-fronted cases holding several bizarre and exotic objects, none of which the man could identify at a glance. Before him at the end of the corridor stood a dressmaker's model clothed in well-used adventurer's garb with a wealth of weapons and other odds and ends on shelves above it. As the dark man stared, he swore the figure moved slightly into a defensive posture. Then the young man walking before him spoke.

"Thank you for coming, Magus. Time is short, and the end is well past nigh at this point. He has refused any nourishment until your arrival. He claims that a clear system will help yield a clear conscience."

"In his case, I doubt it. Clarity to Cinneaus was a tool, like all others. But I am honored at the call. I would have thought he would have had his choice of prelates at his beck and had no need for a lowly parish clerk to help carry him over. But let us not speak ill of the ill in his own house. Lead on and let me do what I can for him."

The Magus was led into a book-filled chamber too small by half for the reputation of the one sprawled across the small wooden camp bed. He was a small and wiry man with a too big nose and a shock of thick gray hair glowing like a nimbus in the guttering of the tallow candles on the scarred desk next to the bed.

"By damned! Boy, I told you to leave me be until the Magus arrived. Had I a flagon, I'd lay what brains you have out like a feast for the bugs! Can't a body even die in peace?"

"Be still, Cinneaus. I am come, though from the sound of things, you have no need for my services except to testify at your trial for homicide."

"Blessed be! Come, Magus. *Boy*! Bring me the decanter of the sweet Rhienish wine and two of the dwarven tankards and whatever flesh the Magus will partake of. Then leave us be unless He calls."

"Now, Cinneaus, you know magi cannot drink of the fruit the vine. Though I would not decline a sizable tankard of ale if you have any on hand. Whatever is at the top of the larder, lad. Make no fuss."

"So be it. A pitcher and tankard of ale and the decanter. Now, go. Talking be work as dry as crossing the Great Sands in summer barefoot. Thank you, child."

Cinneaus took the measure of the Magus during this exchange. Though already feeling the cold breath of death on his face, he was still a man made wise by years of struggle and hard dealings. Making snap judgments on the worth of his fellow man had allowed him to live this long over the course of adventures spanning two continents and careers. The tale he had to tell was going to rattle the Magus to his marrow, and if the man lacked the fortitude to hear it, then Cinneaus would simply have to have the boy seek out another, and he would have to fight death to the last ditch again. The Magus was young enough to be his son, though a good head taller at least. He was emaciated though not malnourished. He felt the man had more than the ordinary degree of both intelligence and cunning, which would serve him well in his station. The jet-black hair and swarthy complexion told of an origin just exotic enough to attract notice from both suitors and likely patrons, but not unusual enough to call his ancestry into question. Cinneaus sighed and locked eyes with the man, just in time to be interrupted by the boy's return with the alcohol.

The Magus named Toulson was new to the island nation of Chorlos and had just been anointed as Vice-Servitor to the Archmagus Philippi of Cheslea, the ruler of both the Mages and the nation itself. He had heard tales about the most famed of the capital's inhabitants since he began his mystical studies under a contemporary and fellow adventurer of the man's named Puckfardt. Puckfardt had told tales of his adventures with a group of freebooting mercenaries in his youth including the antics of an enterprising young thief and trapspolier named Cinneaus. Apparently, the wizened figure before him was the same man, although he was known now as a scholar of darker arts and respected as a squire in Cheslea and a key advisor of the Archmagus. Despite his known impiety and gruff exterior, Cinneaus was worthy of his time and would be a worthy patron, even in death.

"I see you are of Great Loos stock. How is my old friend Puckfardt? Did he ever reclaim the Stone of Scrying, or did he retire back to his farm?"

"What? Eh? I'm sorry." The Mage sputtered around a mouth full of cold-boiled capon with a look of puzzled interest. "Puckfardt? He is dead, sadly. I am unfamiliar with the Stone you speak of. I was his final student and was gifted with his grimoire, but that tool must remain lost. Of course, he spoke highly of you, though I thought you more a thief and trapspolier than a scholar. Of course, you share a name with the Cinneaus who helped clear my native town of Podden of a zombie horde when my grandfather was a boy."

Cinneaus grinned, though it more resembled a rictus than any spark of humor. He had judged the man correctly. The Stone of Scrying was the object of a quest he and Puckfardt had set off on just before their mutual retirement from the active life. A necromancer had decided to add the power of foresight to his repertoire, and the local villagers had decided that enough was enough. It was bad enough to know their late loved ones were being used to gain a madman power, but to have him to be able to see the future clearly was too much.

The promise of keeping anything they could carry from the castle of the necromancer and ten pounds of gold made the decision easy. After slaying the few living underlings about and dismembering about a dozen undead retainers, they arrived face-to-face with the man, a defrocked Magus named Vomhissler who had acquired the knack for reviving the recent dead and the lack of scruples to put the knowledge they retained to use. His plan was to use the Stone of Scrying to track the movements of the then-Arch Magus of Cheslea and attack him when at his weakest during a trip to install Magi in the provinces through the victims of a plague that had recently decimated the Princedom of Fratellum. Upon the death of the Arch Magus, Vomhissler would claim the position by right of conquest.

The only problem was that the Stone only existed in the man's overactive imagination. In fact, the arrival of Cinneaus and Puckfardt sufficed to give the fool a fatal heart attack. Puckfardt decided to move in to the castle and set up as a mentor for Magi, while Cinneaus collected some odds and pieces and his share of the loot and returned to his keep just outside Cheslea. The books triggered an interest in the teaching of a Mosite from the Great Sands named Lazarus and decided the balance of his life's work. Every day he thanked the Gods for allowing him to have a mind quick enough to pick up enough languages to function as a Mage and for having parents who felt literacy was more important even than a trade. Although being trained as a locksmith and trapspolier had made all the rest possible.

"Oh yes, in my youth I was an adept at traps, both the making and breaking of the things. In fact, if you should have to linger here with me overnight, don't wander too far alone. Some of the ones I set up here decades ago are still primed and ready. The last thing I need is another death on my record, even an accidental one. Erebus is already readying her reception for me and the Ankou's wagon rattles ever closer. But, the fate of Puckfardt is not what brought you here or led to the summons. And I am the same Cinneaus.

"'Twas then I first met good Puckfardt. But no back-glancing. I am dying. Too many years banging about in dungeons, too many potions sampled, too many wenches bedded, and too many books have caught up to me. But I have cause to confess, and I have a revelation that may serve an ambitious man like yourself, if you can forgive the source. And yes, you are ambitious. I've seen that light in other men's eyes, including my own. Vice-Servitor is an excellent starting point, but not much of a finish. No, you seek bigger things. Sadly, the days of questing have passed for most, but you may be able to go as yet depending on what you do with my offering."

"Sir, you judge me too harsh. I am in service to the gods and to the Arch Magus, not to you. I am ambitious, but not overly or above my place. You should have had the Arch Magus come. He is of a station to hear—"

"*Shut up.* No one is here but you, me, and my boy. The boy is my son Herne. Do not discount him. He chose you of the entire staff of the Arch Magus. Besides, if the Arch Magus heard my tale, he'd have me cut to strips by the dawn's breaking and mixed into the mortar of the extension of the city walls. Now, will you listen and learn? Or is my boy a far worse judge of character than I have taught him to be?"

After that outburst, Cinneaus was wracked by a coughing fit that shook the bedframe. On the shout, the boy stuck his head in and stared daggers at the Mage. The Mage, in turn, blushed and waved the boy away. He was ashamed for how well Cinneaus had nailed his ambition, but he decided to humor the old man. A patron like this was a once in a lifetime chance, and the son's gratitude might be even better than the father's.

Between gagging, hacking coughs, Cinneaus smiled inwardly. The Mage was already convinced. Beyond the ten percent tithe-offering of his estate for his service, the chance to gain knowledge known by no one else was too tasty a lure to spit out. Besides, Herne's skills as an alchemist would make replacing the tithe-offering child's play. And if the Arch Magus decided to take umbrage at the news Cinneaus passed on, Herne's position as Councilor of Chorlos and heir to Toria Priory and connections with other realms would insulate him from any frontal attacks.

"Very well, speak on. But first, let me perform the necessary rites in case *your* ambition outruns your mortal spark."

With that, the Mage pulled a mirror of black basalt and a dull dagger of pure iron from under his sea-green robe and approached the foot of the bed.

"Remove the bedclothes, please, and any garments." Toulson knew Cinneaus was nude under the light linen sheet and woolen campaign blanket, but he also knew that the niceties must be upheld. Upon the unveiling of the figure before him, Toulson blanched, even though he had served the same duty for plaque victims in three different parishes in the last eighteen months. No living man had this many scars and still lived. His torso was a mass of slashes, gashes, and what could only be teeth marks. Scars of battlefield stitches marked his arms and legs. His thin chest was pockmarked with punctures both large and small. The knees and ankles too showed signs of rough wear and a total lack of connective tissue. The fact that Cinneaus needed to be helped over was not a shock, but the fact that he had lasted this long was. However, after a second or two, the Mage regained his footing and continued. He traced over every old wound with the dull dagger, drawing out any remaining pain into the iron so the Lodestone could remove it later, and scribbled them all down on the vellum scroll for transcription by the scribe onto the Silver Scroll. Upon completion of this chore, the Mage drew a reed with a burnt end out of his robe's collar and drew a small circle on the pulse point of the older man's wrist for the Exsauingator. He did note and linger over the missing middle finger on the old man's left hand, which brought forth the following cryptic comment, which the Mage merely nodded in response to.

"Oddsen gave an eye for knowledge, but I merely lost a finger for far greater."

First the examination of the body had to be complete so that the gods knew what errors or damage to correct on the resurrection before the body was reborn and written up on the Silver Scroll for burial. Then the examination of the soul was to follow. This is what the mirror was for. It was to be placed on the chest of the dying man and would catch his confession word for word. Later, back at the Arch Magus's palace, a scribe would use the appropriate spells to transcribe the words onto the reverse of the scroll. This helped guide the gods in placing the soul and body together into the proper place in the afterlife. Though to Toulson's thinking, Cinneaus was destined for Elysium as surely as any defender of the faith or Arch Mage.

"Speak of who you are and of whom you are come, please," the Mage said to the raspily breathing figure prone before him. The prominent breastbone held the mirror like a grooved stand.

"I am Cinneaus of Ulm, Lord of Toria Priory and father of Herne of Cheslea. I am the only child of Berrius and Toria, freeholders of Ulm. I have been an adventurer, trap maker and trap breaker, locksmith and a scholar. I am also a Lazarite."

Toulson drew still. Lazarite? What fresh heresy was this? He had heard from Puckfardt that some adventurers returned from far lands with more than social diseases and booty to burn. Some returned with strange new ideas and ways to reorder society to better serve themselves. He had written it off as the ramblings of an old man, bored with his now sedentary ways, but Cinneaus was the first adventurer he had served in this fashion. The Mage regained his poise and continued with the ceremony.

"Justify your existence and why the gods should not use you as cosmic fertilizer in the Gardens of Paradise."

"I have served the Gods in my own fashion. I have dispatched many evil men to Erebus and filled the Ankou's cart with their remnants. I have offered sacrifices out of joy and duty. I have kept the faith and obeyed the gods to the best of my ability. Should I speak on or will that do for the scribes?"

"Yes, that will be plenty. The gods should grant you the boon of eternal life and happiness at their bosom," the Mage said and removed the mirror, returning both it and the dagger to their pouch in his purse. "Now, what, pray tell, is a Lazarite?"

"Directness from a Mage? It is a true wonder! I must be dying because that is one of the signs of the end. All in good time, my sage friend, but first a tale. Do you recall the crusade that Arch Magus Nicanor the Third called about forty years back? Of course not, your father must have been a mere babe in those distant days. At any rate, the Mosite pirates had cut off trade with the Reboh coast of the Sudten Mere. Nicanor, who was a native Rebohite and whose family had made its fortune trading slaves with the Mosites, issued the call and coupled it with a Grand Forgiving, meaning that any who died in the conflict would be forgiven all sins and allowed to proceed directly to Paradise whether or not a Mage was handy. Puckfardt and I were still at Podden, recovering from our clash with the zombies when the word arrived. We had hit it off and decided to take part, especially when it was mentioned that any booty claimed under right of conquest would be exempt from tithing. We were young and greedy, not impious, mind. We gathered up a few locals and the rest of our party of adventurers and set sail for Shihor, which was merely a three-day sail, and we thought would be the natural rendezvous for the Crusade, since it was leaving from Chorlos. We were about a dozen, half of whom were brave boys from Podden who crewed the boat, myself and Puckfardt, a Priest of Erebus named Leevus whom no one trusted until *after* the fighting was done, two Elven wenches who could outfight most men and hold their own between the sheets after, and a Dwarf named Thunk who favored an Orc's club about as tall as he was. Thunk spent the voyage hanging over the rail and cursing everybody who got within hearing distance. Puckfardt and I spent the trip either bedding the wenches or talking about magic. The encounter with the zombies had again piqued my interest and Puckfardt decided to practice his teaching skills on me. The reason for my renewed interest was the fresh and livid scar on my chest caused by a magical trap I couldn't disarm that sent an enchanted crossbow bolt straight through me. Leevus had healed me back to the point I could use my sling right after, but I cursed my own ignorance and hoped to pick up enough to avoid a repeat anytime soon. Being alive in death was no pleasure trip, boy; let no one tell you different. He taught me a spell to detect dark magic, which he felt would serve us well against the Mosites and their disdain for the Pantheon and embrace of the Unity in its place. Of course, things never run straight when adventurers go on a romp. Just before we hit the harbor at Shihor, Scarlett, the Elven wench I had been taking up with since before Podden, took offense at a clumsy game of grab-ass by one of the local boys and threw the stupid bastard overboard. To quell the incipient mutiny, we had to barter the boat back to the folks from Podden instead of selling it for scrap and supplies. Oh well, ride the tiger and some days you get bit."

Here the Mage interjected quietly. "He was my great-uncle. Mother always said his smaller head ruled his large one."

"Sorry for your loss, but Scar always was…touchy about her person. Of course, we got to Shihor before the rest of the army. Too many seamstresses tugging at corners make for a short quilt. So we had two choices: wait or strike out for Reboh on our own and do what damage we could do. Of course, going first would give us the best chance for both glory and booty, so that won easily. The party, now down to the half dozen of us, invaded the Hempen Necklace tavern just off the harbor to supply for our jaunt into the Great Sands. Leevus wandered off to find a Temple to re-consecrate his holy items and to get some more healing potions and components for mixing more since we did seem to run through his supplies awfully fast. Scarlett and her friend Arabella went to purchase more arrows and other odds and ends. Thunk found a spot at the bar and began to drain the town's supply of ale to drought levels, while Puckfardt and I began to restock our larders and find transport. With the gifts of silk and wool we had received from the grateful folks in Podden, we decided we could play at being cloth traders bound for Kefar. Kefar was the main trading hub on the Sudten Mere and just a day's ride south of Reboh, so it would make us a bit less conspicuous than riding straight into Reboh with blades swinging. Of course, we would have to convince the ladies to…conceal some of their best features to my mind, as they would be taken for slaves and treated as such otherwise. Camels were acquired with ease, though with much haggling, as is the way with those Sudteners. Shihor was known for its bargains, if one had the stamina to strike one. We led the beasts back to the tavern and called the rest of the party to our shared chamber on the third floor.

"The ladies objected in violent terms to the prospect of denying who they were, but the prospect of rich booty and much bloodshed soon smoothed their feathers. Thunk was in no real condition to argue, though his disdain for any transport but shank's mare was well known. Leevus readily agreed. Too readily in retrospect. We agreed to mount up and set off at first light. Thunk collapsed into a drunk as prodigious as any tried by Silenus and Leevus left us to pray for our success at his temple. Puckfardt and I decided to complete the pantomime by getting the correct, but well-forged, papers from an old friend of long acquaintance. The last thing we needed was some ambitious sentry or watchman detaining us and allowing the Crusaders to get to Reboh ahead of us. The vultures would have better luck than we in that instance. But Sahmeen could fool the gods into letting the dead walk if told how the paperwork should look first.

"Sahmeen met us at the door of his hut just south of the Plaza of the Ebon Blade, the main temple in Shihor. Neither Puckfardt nor I knew or cared much about the lore of Shihor, but we had heard horror tales in backrooms over the years about the rites of the Ebon Blade to not be tempted into trespassing. Sahmeen swept us both into his long arms and fussed over us like prodigals returned. We could not speak until we had each choked back a cup of tea so sweet we each lost a tooth on smelling it. After wading through a small ocean of verbiage, I told Sahmeen that we needed passes to Kefar for six cloth traders. He spat into the corner and fixed his hawk-like eye on us. He warned us about going beyond Kefar as the Mosite Patriarch had gone mad with power and closed off Reboh to strangers due to the 'fool of an infidel of an Arch Magus.' His words, not mine, mind."

"But of course. And hospitality and discretion led you not to argue the point," said the Magus with a slight smirk.

"Of course. But Sahmeen willingly created passes suitable for royalty that would suit even the most suspicious zealot. We chatted about past exploits for an hour or so, but Puckfardt and I left on hearing the call to worship. Some places are not safe, even for brave and experienced adventurers. We returned to the Hempen Necklace in time to intervene in a good old-fashioned bar brawl caused by Thunk being moved off his bar stool and rudely tossed into a corner table of Dushkite whores. Thunk broke the tankard of ale he had only drank half of over their pimp's head when he objected. This served as the opening bell for a general melee. Puckfardt cast a sleep spell over everybody but the five of us, as Leevus had not yet returned, and we headed upstairs to pack for our departure.

"In the morn, Leevus met us at the bar, and we paid for the damages of the night before and settled our account. No adventurer wants to lose the prospect of a good bed and a safe haven. We then headed off for Kefar in our usual order. I led, having been to Kefar before and being a known person in the area. Scarlett and Arabella came next, arrows notched under long red robes. Leevus rode next wondering all over our tracks as he half-meditated and half-slept, followed by Puckfardt with our pack train of three extra camels. We were waved through at the border after only a cursory glance at our papers. The gold piece did help grease those skids as well though. We made good time, and due to the full moon, we decided to keep pressing on to Reboh hoping to use the night to our advantage. Would that I had chosen to sleep instead! Just before dawn, we arrived at the suburbs of Reboh, or their remains at least. The Patriarch had decided to pursue a scorched-Earth policy and had burnt everything that could not be moved inside the city gates. At the smoldering ruins of a shepherd's hovel, we decided to refine our plan of attack. None of us were keen on attacking a city full of zealots crazed enough to burn their own property. Of course, that was when everything went to Erebus like a stone rolling down a mine-shaft. First, Scarlett had to make water, so she wandered away from the rest of us…right into a group of drunken sentries. No sooner than she revealed her sex did they close in on her and offer several helpful suggestions for better uses for that pearl of great price. The ringleader got a dagger in the throat for his trouble. The other three grabbed her as she hissed and scratched like a rabid tomcat. The noise attracted our attention, so we fell on them en masse. Puckfardt caught a baton in the side of the head early on and went down like a load of hay had been dropped on him. I repaid the baton wielder with a ball to the paunch. Arabella took a crossbow bolt to the throat and bled out before I could scream for Leevus to tend to her. Scarlett kicked the poor bastard who shot Arabella in the face and caved his nose in. He choked to death gasping in a pool of bloody snot. Thunk smashed the poor fool who had just recovered from my sling ball with his club and sprayed us all with the contents of his head, rotten as they were. Leevus finally made his presence known by blowing a packet of hellsbane into the melee, freezing all of us like statuary in the Garden of Sharadite the Snake-tressed. My last memory of the man was a chuckle as he collected his payment for services rendered to the odd man out. The fifth man was far too pale to be a Mosite and stood a head taller than Leevus, who had that much height over me. With a gesture, two carts came out of the main gate of the city, and we were loaded up like rubbish. The natives, of course, segregated from us interlopers.

"I came to in a cell, though not the dungeon hole I feared. It was fairly large and had room for three cots, two stools, and a desk, and if not for the barred window and brazen door, I would have thought the events of the dawn a bad dream. Puckfardt sat on the stool in the far corner from me, holding his head gingerly around a huge goose egg just behind his right ear. Scarlett seemed to be intact as she slept on the cot opposite me, still wearing her red travelling robe. She slept, though I knew any further motion or noise from me would cause her to spring up into a fighting stance. Thunk was the only one of us restrained, chained to the wall at the ankle with a chain longer than he was tall. I chuckled at our predicament and decided to brave any intruding ears. 'Well, folks, what a fine crew we are. Fooled by a prayer-mumbler and locked up like falcons before the hunt in a gilded cage. How fare we all? I see Puckfardt pushing his brains back in to his head, but the rest of us seem to be in one piece. Now, what do we do and how do we avenge sweet Arabella?' Thunk spoke up. 'You have slept for two full days, short one. Much has passed in your absence through the Gate of Bone. Arabella has gone to Paradise alright. These…monsters burnt her last night as an offering to the Unity. Leevus is a damned traitor. He sold us out in Shihor for thirty pearls and the profit made on our sale. He walks at the side of the tall man like a pup follows a boy with a crust. I heard his nasally sing-song preside over the offering of Arabella. May Erebus tear his liver out for a lamp wick for his damned treachery.' At this, Scarlett blanched and growled through tears, 'I will eat his testicles in a stew before I pass over. His heart will adorn me like a diadem.' I had seen the woman fight; grin you not, Mage, she was capable of that and worse. She was no mere wench for pleasures in the dark of a chamber but a true warrior. Thunk continued, 'The tall man is called Davut and is the High Priest of the Unity. He is of Chloron stock, a noble to hear him speak. The Patriarch fawns on his every word, and I think the man wants to return to Chloros and rule in Nicanor's place. Hence the increase in the piracy and the anger of the Arch Mage. Davut wished to speak to you when you recovered your wits as the leader of our motley crew of misfits, since Leevus told him this trip was entirely your conception.'"

"I expect Puckfardt took objection to that," interjected Toulson. "Given that I had heard from him that Reboh trip was a mutual decision."

"It was at that. But let me—" Here another violent coughing fit seized the old man, causing the entire bed to shake like the Last Culling was at hand. "Finish. But first, pray pour me another tankard full. The wine keeps the demon cough at bay."

"Puckfardt merely groaned as Thunk spoke, then said quietly, 'Aye, Cinneaus, I too told Davut that you bore the blame, since I thought you came through our visit with the locals in less hurt than I. And I know how high your pain threshold is. When you are ready, you are to bang on the door thrice to have him summoned.'

"'Ah,' I said brightly. 'Here is a good omen. We can strike him down when he enters and go find and dispose of the dung that is Leevus and bend the Patriarch to our wills.'

"Here our scheming died aborning for Davut himself entered bearing a tray of bread, cheeses, and a pitcher of the watery fig brandy favored by Mosites since the fruit of the vine is forbidden them. 'I thought I heard more voices in the choir when I last passed,' the tall man said as if we were all chatting over breakfast at some wayside inn. ''Tis good to see you awake, Cinneaus. We need to speak privately when you and yours have dined. I would join you, but somehow I feel my presence might hinder conversation.'

"The damned fiend must be a Planeswalker. How else could he have known what we were plotting? And why are we together? No other dungeon I've been in allows the like. This is all passing strange. Then even I fell silent as hunger stabbed my belly and the aroma of the fresh bread seduced me and the others. We ate like what we were for all rights, condemned men and women in the shadow of the Axeman. As Scarlett poured the dregs of the pitcher into her mug, I stood and strode to the door.

"She looked up at me with the nearest she could come to pity. 'I trust you will not sell us cheaply if at all. I will mourn you and then avenge you if I must. *But*, if you betray us, you will die at my hands, either in this life or the next.' I kissed her violently and told her that she would have no need to whet her blade on my account. With a nod at the others, I struck the door with a closed fist three times. No sooner than the ringing from the third blow had faded, Davut opened the door himself. I entered the corridor showing more bravery than I felt. I fully expected to feel the blades of henchmen slice into me before the door closed to my rear. Instead, Davut smiled and bade me to follow him to the stairway at the end of the corridor. 'I only discuss business in the light of the sun. Talk indoors tends to limit one's thoughts to the worldly, and we have higher topics to cover.' With that, he motioned me to lead on up the stairway. After two switchbacks, we arrived at a rope ladder hanging from a skylight in the roof. I stole a glance down the maw of the stairwell below and counted at least five landings before the darkness engulfed my field of vision. I exited onto a pavement of blue and white mosaic. Two wooden chairs stood beside a small round table, and I could see the far distant Sudten Mere gleaming to the west. I noticed with some distaste the wide grate behind one of the chairs just as Davut bade me to sit in that very chair.

"'So you are the famed Cinneaus. Trapspoiler, adventurer, and sometime seeker of knowledge. I had thought you would be taller. I must warn you, though I am unarmed, I am not defenseless, and I doubt you wish to trade your cell for the oubliette below.' I shook my head as the charnel stench rose to my nostrils. 'Now, do me the boon of spreading your left hand on the table beside you.' I did as he asked, and before I could blink, the middle finger on my hand was severed by a steaming blade. The wound was sealed as fast as it had been caused. I neither screamed nor bled a drop. 'Knowledge comes at a cost, and yours has been paid. Now, let me speak to you of the Lazarites.'"

Here Toulson leaned forward. The recitation of adventures older than he on top of two tankards of the strong but sweet wine had begun to lull him to a waking sleep. Finally, the meat he had been waiting for. He discreetly pulled the mirror from his purse and sat it on his lap inside his sleeve as Cinneaus spoke on.

"'You think I am here to foment a rebellion in Chloros and seize the Arch Mage's throne while he sates his bloodlust on mere pirates. Bah! I have no interest in worldly power. I wish to replace the misguided fools like the Arch Mage and the Patriarch and their false beliefs with the *truth*. Have you heard of Jehu, the Prophet of the Great Sands?'

"When confronted by madness on a monumental scale, always play dumb. Madmen find their own voice to be more soothing than music. So I answered in the affirmative. Jehu was known all over the world as a great prophet and teacher. He was, of course, wrong; especially when he denounced the gods as mere myths and make believe. Of course, the question needed no answer. At least not that Davut could hear.

"'Jehu was a great man, but he was the merest herald to the *true one*. Did you know a man can lie three days dead and live again? Do you know a man can tell of what is to come and what has been after so doing? What price would you pay above what you already have for that knowledge?'

"Here I had to pause. Necromancy was not a topic I enjoyed. Far too many of my troubles lay at the feet of fools who sought to commune over-long with the dead. Now, I knew that man could seem to be dead for all practical points and live again if the right potion in the right hands was forthcoming. I had myself done that more than once. But to be truly dead and then truly live again? I trod close to blasphemy and swallowed.

"'I would pay dear for that knowledge, as would any man. Who has not sought to learn from one's ancestors or sought to teach those to come? But that of which you speak is impossible. The dead may walk again, but they are even then in death's embrace. Hence the need for both fire and scattering to rid oneself of them. To truly live again? I cannot see how.'

"Ah, the one you call Leevus is the One. He was known as Lazarus of Olivet before Jehu came to him. Jehu offered to teach him the True Way to Paradise, and he accepted. Sadly, Jehu was called away by his father, and Lazarus grew ill with a wasting disease in his absence. The daughters of Lazarus were afflicted with greed for their inheritance and strangled their father while he slept in isolation from the rest of the house. He was prepared as the Mosites do their dead and sealed in a rock tomb.'

"Here I shuddered. 'Entombment? How horrible. Far better to be sealed in lead and made ready for the Culling intact.'

"'But weep not. Jehu returned, and on the third day inquired for Lazarus. The daughters, making ready for their marriages, told Jehu that Lazarus was dead and entombed already. Jehu knew the truth and summoned Lazarus from the tomb. He did so and left with Jehu by another way. He changed his name to Leevus and wandered in search of a worthy heir for his knowledge. I am that man. But, I grow old, and I am weary of the fruitlessness of my task. I bid you take my place and learn all that can be taught by Lazarus.'

"'Had it been any other, I would do so gladly. But I am sworn with the rest of my party to see Leevus dead for his betrayal of us. The sacrifice and disposal of poor Arabella alone makes vengeance a necessity. So I must ask you return me to my cell and then do what thou willst to me and mine. Honor forbids any other option. Then I sat quietly as he turned my words over in his mind. I was tempted but he knew what my choice would be."

'Very well. The die has been cast. I will escort you back to the rest of your party and will come for you later. You will have another guest this evening at your service.' And with that, we returned to the cell where he left me with what almost passed for disappointment.

"My return intact and in deep thought sparked much interest amongst my friends. Scarlett forced Puckfardt to cast a rudimentary truth-telling spell on me in order to ascertain that my survival was not bought with information Davut had no cause to know or at the price of their lives or freedom. She kept me at arm's length for the rest of the night, even after I passed to the satisfaction of the others. I told them what had transpired, which brought forth rousing denunciations from Thunk and a mere shake of the head from Puckfardt. I knew Puckfardt was most disappointed in me for my refusal than anything else, so it was to him I justified my decision.

"'Friend Puckfardt, you of all the rest know my burning desire for knowledge, especially that which it is not my place to know. It is one of, if not the main motive for my jaunts into dangers like this one. Erebus himself could not conceive of a better snare for me than Davut did. *But* my first loyalty is and always will be to my fellows regardless of the costs to myself. Have I ever abandoned you, even when logic and prudence would so demand? So, why should I do so now? Now, Thunk, I ask the same of you. Are my actions of the past few hours so out of character? Many is the hour we have fought hordes back-to-back past all endurance for far less than vengeance. Let us be patient. Our unwelcoming host seems to be greater than his parts, so let us see what boons the gods give us overnight. If we all survive 'til first light, then we will make better plans.'

"Well, we had no need to tarry in suspense. At the supper hour, Davut did not come with our victuals. Instead, Leevus entered our chamber. He was empty-handed and shorn of his priestly robes. He came in only a loincloth and bore signs of having been severely chastised before his coming to us. Scarlett was upon him before the door even closed. To his credit, he took his beating like a man and never even flinched, even when she castrated him barehanded. To be given such a gift was just what her mood needed. His moans brought the gleam that had been missing since the death of Arabella back to her cat-like green eyes. When she allowed him to collapse and crawl into the farthest corner to whimper to himself, she curled up on her cot and licked his blood from her fingertips. I had to lighten the mood, so I asked, 'Does the taste of him suit you better than I?' With a feral grin, she shook her head no and winked at me, as lewdly as any drunken sailor in a cathouse with ready gold in hand. The other two just shook their heads, though Thunk did wander over to the poor thing and kick him in the face for a minute or two, until a voice from the corridor interrupted his pleasure just as Puckfardt rose to get his licks in.

"'Come forth, the lot of you, at *once*.' There was no doubt that Davut was summoning us for reasons unknown. We all entered the hall in campaign order and in defensive postures: myself, Scarlett, Puckfardt, and Thunk to the rear. Davut stood at the near end of the hall with our gear behind him. 'I hope you enjoyed my gift to you. Upon learning that he had betrayed you into my hands, I decided that he was an unworthy tool, and if he would be comrades-in-arms for a mere pottage of jewels, then what price would I bring? Now, Cinneaus, step forward and buy the freedom of your fellows.'

"'What price do you demand? My honor is no commodity and surely my loyalty is not yours to call on. You have my worldly goods at your command. What else do you desire?'

"'That you merely step forward and listen to the words I offer for your ears alone. After the hearing, what you do with them is your decision alone. *Now come!*

"At that, my feet moved of their own volition towards the tall man. Scarlett saw my reluctance and made to pull me back, but at a gesture from Davut, the others were flung through the air like parchment in a breeze. This got my temper up, and I fought the forces compelling me as much as I could. The walk of a dozen paces seemed to take a moon or more. When I was face-to-chest with Davut, he stooped to my level, squatting like he was approaching a privy. He leaned forward on the balls of his feet and whispered the following in my ear, 'You are a worthy heir to the powers of Lazarus, even more than the man himself. You will gain that which you seek, but only when it will serve you no good purpose. We will meet again at your ending and you will tell me what is to be.' With that, he rose to his full height and vanished. No sooner than he departed were the others at my side asking what had just occurred. I told them what he had said and shrugged as it was gibberish more suited to the stage than conversation and made as much sense.

"That was my last campaign. We left Reboh just before the crusade arrived, and it fell in an orgy of blood and flame, but due to Davut's generosity, we left with all manner of gold and jewels and...other items after we cleaned out the palace. The Mosites offered us no resistance as we returned up the coastal road to Shihor. I have oft wondered in quiet moments if Davut marked us in some way to allow us safe passage because even the blind could tell we were not natives. Scarlett and I decided to return to Toria together, and we were together for the next decade in great happiness. Of course, without benefit of any true ceremony, she was free as she had been born, and one day I awoke to an empty bed and a note reading 'Life calls. Take care 'til the Culling and raise our son well. I have loved you as well as I could, and I know you have as well. Until the next.' That note has rested next to my heart until your coming. Yes, Herne knows of his mother. I expect he will seek her out once the anchor of me is tossed over the side. You know more of Puckfardt's fate than I. But I hope he was happy with his lot. Thunk left us in Shihor. Simply gathered his goods and took off on the next ship. Again I hope his chosen lot was a happy one. The rest of me you have either heard the truth of or the lies that grow in one's absence. Now, Mage, what questions have you for the Ankou is come and is impatient to remove his load?"

"By the Gods, what is a Lazarite? An hour of talk and no answer. I could return to school and get the same and not wear out new sandals in the hearing! Palaver Palaver!"

As Toulson rose, he forgot the mirror in his haste. To his shock, the old man reached out and grabbed it before it landed on the flagstones below.

"A Lazarite *knows* what lies beyond. You think this is my first taste of death, fool? I hope this to be the last. As I said, potions work wondrously well in the right hands. I have spoken to the dead on three continents. From charnel houses to battlefields, from plague pits to the deathbeds of noble maids in childbirth. Every time I have returned, gasping and retching, the faces of those I have loved and lost and even dispatched with malice aforethought stare back. All tell the same tale. A great void. Just you and the darkness. Nothing else. We all arrive in different ways and with different burthens, but we all arrive nonetheless. All this gimcrackery with mirrors and daggers and burnt offerings serve only to soothe the living. The dead are no longer. We merely wait. For what none knows, but we wait, just like we do here. My boy will see you down. I am thankful for your help, as it was freely given in faith, and I hope it will soothe me as time devours all before me until the Great Ending comes for all. With that said, I passed the help of any option or spell. This then is the final death, the True One even. I welcome it like a lover."

With that final outburst, Cinneaus pulled the sheet up over his head and turned towards the wall, and his raspy breathing finally ceased.

Herne dashed in and escorted the Mage out, profusely thanking him for coming both materially and verbally. The Mage nodded and made a gesture of blessing the boy, the place, and the dead within, though he knew that the Arch

Magus would not be pleased at his reporting. So engrossed in thought was he that he paid no mind to the tall blond-haired man who trudged up to the gate of Toria and rang the bell lugging an empty handcart. The Ankou looked over his shoulder at the retreating Mage and whispered, "Soon enough, you will see that Davut spoke truly and so did Cinneaus."

THE LAST HOUSE
ON THE PAVEMENT

Now, Early September:

"DAMNIT! ANOTHER TENANT DONE RUN OFF!"

George Herbert was not pleased. As the leading real estate man in Hemphill, he prided himself on his ability to read folks. The Grant Wylies came from outstanding stock, and he knew that Grant's sainted granddaddy never believe that his boy had just cut and run. Even from a haint like the one on Lowell Drive. The boy was made of sterner stuff. It had to be the girl's fault. Cheslea Falls wasn't exactly quality, and she wasn't from what passed for it in those parts. Hell, she was half-Yankee to boot. He'd call Miss Nita on Monday and see where they went and get his last month's rent at least. Of course, it would have to be daggum raining cats and dogs. Putting a new "For Rent" sign up could wait until Monday, too.

Then:

THE DEMOCRAT SPINNING MILL IN HEMPHILL OPENED WITH ALL MANNER

of ceremonies on the first of May 1924. The last living Confederate veteran in all of Hemphill County, Colonel Richmond Woods of Kennesaw Mountain and Rivers Bridge fame, cut the ribbon and rang the bell to start the first workday. The mill's owner, Senator Emerson Hoar of Massachusetts, made an appropriate speech and immediately boarded the train right after. To anyone's knowledge, it was his first and only visit to his pride and joy and biggest moneymaker.

Among those going to work on that first-ever second shift was Carl Kimball. His newlywed wife, Gladys, would go in on the first shift on the next day. Carl was a "doffer" and a dang good one, and Gladys ran a loom. The house they moved into, at a payment of two dollars per month, was located at 133 Lowell Drive. It was the first house either of them had ever lived in with a paved road in front of it, even if the blacktop did stop right in front of their place. The house was small, only four rooms: living room, kitchen, and two bedrooms at the back of the house. They had a garage stall off the back alley that was shared with their neighbors on both sides. Since Carl didn't have a car yet, he used it as a makeshift barn for their mule and coop for their yardbirds. The yard wasn't big enough for a real good garden, but Carl took the mule if he had to go any farther than the mill gate. Besides, hooking up the plow on Saturdays and planting a few rows of things reminded him of home back in north Georgia. The work was tough in the plant though. Ten hour days, despite the eight he was promised when the man talked his pappy into letting him come to work, were enough. But the straight-through working and having to eat at the machine threw Carl off. Like many a man before and since, when Carl got off-kilter, some kind soul offered him a jug to get him back to level. And like many a woman before and since, the deeper Carl swam in the jug of White Lightning, the better the first man that didn't drink, and cuss, and slap her when things went sideways looked. In Gladys' case, this man was her supervisor, Tommy deGraff.

Good old Tommy deGraff was born and bred in Hemphill and came from the gentry. Of course, after the War, the deGraffs lost everything but their name. But Tommy was a man about town and hail fellow well met, so he managed to get on the board at the local Savings Bank and drew a steady salary. In his younger days, he was a bit of a radical, going so far as to marry the teacher from the local black prep school, the Garrison Institute. Now he wasn't crazy; she was a white girl and from up in Ohio. She acted like she had sense and some money and with her being as pretty as a French dancer, Tommy was hooked. The only real problem with Miss Lucille was that she was as frigid as the entire ice plant down by Bull Run Creek. I mean, Queen Victoria and Carry Nation would advise her to relax and do her duty. But she didn't. Tommy decided to take the job overseeing the first shift at the new spinning mill because it offered a bit more money and access to a bunch of pretty young naïve farm girls, ripe for the picking. The two percent ownership stake didn't hurt any either.

Things were fine for about four years for the Kimballs. Then Carl decided to start running shine on the weekends and drinking anytime he wasn't working. Gladys, having kept her figure after having two babies (the girl died a-coming, but the boy was just fine), decided that she needed some companionship who would pay her some attention with more than the back of their hand. Tommy noticed her longing glances and decided to see if he would be of any help.

From a few quick clinches in the broom closet to her and Carl's marital bed was a short and quick trip. The next year was as pleasant for Gladys as any she'd known in Hemphill. She had a good man who was good in ways that Carl wasn't on the sly. Carl was so drunk most of the time he had no idea what was happening, and Tommy was making noises about giving up on Miss Lucille and taking off for Florida with her. Then the world turned upside down.

At the Labor Day picnic put on by the Hemphill United Methodist Church, Gladys realized that, although the midwife had said she couldn't have no more babies after the girl was born breeched and choked on the cord, she hadn't had a period in two months. She slipped a note scribbled on the back of a campaign flyer to Tommy asking him to see her at home after their shift the next day. Carl, who was illiterate, saw Gladys write the note and figured out real quick what was up. He decided to lay out of work and circle back home and run Tommy off with whatever kind of persuasion it took. Then he'd settle up with Gladys. Carl was done with the mill. The dust choked him. The bosses had made sell his mule after a neighbor woman bellyached about it eating up her flower bulbs. He was in hock to the company store for more than he was worth living or dead. His pappy was sick over in Georgia and was a-needing Carl to get home at any rate and take up the farm. Gladys would come or just get left. Tomorrow was going to be the day of days. A whole mess of greens was about to get fixed but good.

The events of the first Tuesday in September Nineteen and Twenty-Eight on Lowell Lane would echo through time and space like the vibration of a Chinese gong. First, Tommy and Gladys threw all caution the wind and left the mill together, side-by-side and talking as they walked. Several hands saw them together. It took a good size chunk of old man Hoar's money to make them forget it by the inquest. They walked into the little house at the end of Lowell and made their way to the master bedroom.

Their coming was noticed by Carl, who was in the garage sharpening his axe. He had made a point to be seen toting his axe inside several times so as not to be suspicious. After giving the lovers time to get prepared, he left the garage and circled the far side of the house to the front porch. Having had about half a jug of liquid courage, Carl paused and caught his wind, then kicked the shut front door in. He heard two voices and walked towards them. They showed no sign of noticing his arrival in the least. The two brazens had even left the damn door open to the bedroom. Carl thanked the Lord that his boy was still at vacation bible school and would be spared the shame of it all. He entered the bedroom just in time to hear Gladys say, "It must be yours. I haven't laid with the sot in over a year." She was lying on top of the quilt her momma made for her and Carl as a wedding present as naked as the day she was born. The other man, who Carl knew as a boss at the mill, had his shirt and collar off and his pants unbuttoned. Carl swung the axe at him and caught Tommy flush in the middle of the back. Gladys took a second to notice, and it took the spray of blood hitting her face for her to grasp what was going on. About that time, Carl's second swing took Tommy's head off at the chin. The man fell what would have been face-first across Gladys' legs, freezing her in place as her second scream escaped. There would be no third. Carl swung once more and took off Gladys' head and her right hand. Then he dropped the gore-stained axe across the foot of the bed and took off his blood-soaked clothes. He walked to the closet and took out his church-going overalls and clean white church shirt and redressed. He did clean out Tommy's pockets, getting all of five dollars for his efforts. Then he strolled out the back door to the train station like a man without a care in the world and bought a ticket to Greenwood. From there, he'd buy a ticket up to Toccoa and then walk on back home.

Of course, the screams of a woman coming from a house in the middle of the afternoon tend to attract attention. And given Carl's habits over the last little while, folks tended to watch him with a sideways look as he was a mite unpredictable. A man known to be broke and with no ready cash buying a train ticket also focuses folks' attention. Hence, Carl barely got his ticket bought before the chief of police in Hemphill walked up behind him and said, "Boy, one of your neighbors called up and said your missus was raising all kinds of Cain a few minutes ago. Then things got quiet and you left and calm-like. Now, we both know no woman ever let a man have the last word if she's awake. So, let's you and me ride back to your place and see what needs to be."

Carl looked at him with a blank stare. He knew he couldn't go back to that house. He said to the chief, "Sir, I just got a letter saying my pappy is bad sick back in Georgia. Gladys said she couldn't go with me cause of work, so I admit, I roughed her up some and knocked her out. Let me go see about my pappy, and I will see you in about a week if she files any paper on me. I don't expect pappy to live. Please, sir, as a feller Christian."

The chief rubbed his stubble. This wasn't procedure, but Carl was a good enough fellow sober. Besides, he had let Tommy deGraff go after a talking to the night before for the same thing. Miss Lucille made some wild claims about Tommy and some hussy from the mill and one thing led to another. After the flowerpot took flight, Tommy had clocked her in the jaw for some peace. The chief decided to let the man go on a promise to return. Besides, if the wife insisted, Carl could be picked up in Greenwood just as easy.

"Okay, Carl. Wish your folks well, and I'll pray for your pappy. I lost my daddy last winter, and I know how bad it hits a man. I'll see what the wife wants to do about all this in a bit."

With that, Carl thanked the man and got on the train. After it left the station, the chief had a sudden thought. Carl hadn't had any baggage with him. He asked the ticket agent if Carl had a bag or a case when he got his ticket, and the agent told him no and made a snide comment about how the Catawba and Broad Railway did not allow gunny sacks as checked baggage. The chief decided to go check on Gladys now. He knew the train to Greenwood took about four hours and that a phone call would be enough to get Carl back if needed. He climbed into his A Model and chugged off to the end of Lowell Drive.

Upon his arrival, he cursed his tender heart and tender head in equal measure. The front door was kicked in and the imprint of a muddy size-eleven brogan was dead center. The heartwood pine floors showed evidence of a fresh scratch or scuff from some sharp metal object, so freshly sharpened that metal bits stuck out of the floor every few feet. Now the chief felt his gorge get buoyant. As he entered the bedroom, he threw up two days' worth of good eating. Damn, Miss Lucille was owed an apology after her jaw got unwired. He picked up the phone in the living room and called the operator. He asked for the ambulance from Boylston Hospital and for the train station. He needed to get Carl off that train in Newberry at the soonest.

Well, they brought Carl back to Hemphill and arrested him for double murder. The trial lasted about two hours, and he was found guilty and sentenced to hang at the state prison in Columbia before the end of the year. A bad batch of shine was blamed and the revenuers were called in to do a sweep. Tommy deGraff was painted as a gallant boss gone to take care of an abused employee at her urgent call. Gladys was painted as the longsuffering wife and mother tethered to an abusive lush of a monster who snapped due to Demon Rum. Any evidence to the contrary was either bought off or buried. Miss Lucille saw to the adoption of Gladys and Carl's boy to a nice couple from out of state named Tolson. Carl was hurried off to Columbia and found hung in his cell two weeks after his arrival on his own shirt.

Now, late August:

"**WELL, FOLKS, IT IS A STEAL AND IT'S PERFECT FOR A NEWLYWED COUPLE LIKE** yourselves. Walking distance to the Arts Academy and a nice big lot. Screened-in porch on the front and a quiet neighborhood. For five hundred a month, I'd live there if the wife would let me. So, y'all want to come back by the office in the morning and sign the paperwork and try it out tonight? It is furnished after all."

George Herbert knew this deal was sealed. The offer to stay overnight was just a sweetener. Lisa Wylie had spent the last three hours oohing and ahhing over the little house on Lowell Drive. She had talked to her best girlfriend and mother and sent at least a hundred pictures to them of things she just loved about it. George and Grant Wylie had chatted and smoked on the back porch, lamenting the sorry state of the old garages and the fact that the city of Hemphill had never paved the back alley as it would be a perfect shared driveway. The only blemish on the place was the gouged and scratched heartwood pine floors. Those would need to be stripped and redone before they bought it but, Lisa could hide them under rugs for now. Yes, they'd love to spend the night and would see him at his office about ten. George smiled to himself as he walked back to his Lincoln.

Now, Early September:

THE WYLIES DID STAY THE NIGHT THE LAST NIGHT OF AUGUST IN THE LITTLE house on Lowell. It was cozy and, given they did very little actual sleeping on the pallet they had placed in the larger of the two bedrooms, they were impressed at the homey atmosphere of the place. I mean, they were still newlyweds less than two weeks removed from the wedding after all. The next morning, they called the movers to gather up the stuff from their apartment over in Cheslea Falls and met Mr. Herbert at his office to sign the lease and pick up the other key. The next few days were a frenzy of unpacking and rearranging furniture.

Finally, on Labor Day, they decided to have a housewarming party. They packed the front of the house to the gills with folks. Every family member on both sides who lived within driving distance and every teacher from the district (both Grant and Lisa taught at the high school in Hemphill) came bearing knick-knacks and hand-me-downs. Basically, they got every salad tong and soup spoon they hadn't got off their wedding registry. Grant would have preferred the cash, but Lisa and both their mommas had insisted and that was that. The party was kinda rowdy, especially for a Monday, but that was okay. The last stragglers left about midnight and both the Wylies collapsed into their queen bed and slept two rows at a time until the alarm clock roused them at five a.m. The next day things started to settle into a routine as life does. This lasted about a week and then things went to hell.

The next Tuesday, Grant got roped into proctoring the GED test for the high school. He wasn't thrilled at the prospect of working until ten and getting up at five, but the extra two hundred dollars would come in handy down the road. Meanwhile, Lisa got home just after five and decided to read in bed until Grant got home. He knew he needed to work for the extra money, but she would much rather he be home, especially since she could stand the company. About eight-thirty, it began to get dark, and she decided to get up and find a snack.

While she was in the kitchen, staring into the fridge in hopes of finding some junk food to tide her over until Grant got home with some take-out, she heard the front door fly open and bang against the wall. She squeaked out Grant's name and got no response. She heard something scraping on the floor and grabbed the golf club Grant had left next to the stove "in case she needed it" and slowly crept to the door of the kitchen. The scraping retreated down the hall towards the bedroom she had just left. As she turned into the seemingly empty hall, she noticed the scraping had stopped. She moved the golf club to her shoulder like a baseball bat and prepared to brain whoever was in her new house. As she stepped from the hall, she saw impression of a body on her bed and then saw it bounce violently, like something heavy had just fallen on it. The closet door opened and a mass of cold air moved through her, and within seconds, the back door opened.

Well, that was it for Lisa Wylie and her new house. She grabbed a change of clothes for herself and Grant and went to the high school to wait for Grant out front under the glare of the streetlights. She told him as soon as he left the building what had just happened and made it clear that she wasn't going back to the house on Lowell for love, money, or anything else. He wasn't going back tonight either. They'd get a room over at one of the motels at the exit off I-61 for the rest of the week and pack up on Saturday. There were other places in Hemphill.

Grant just sighed and knew better than to argue with her when she was this upset. When things calmed down in the morning, he'd try to talk some sense into her if he could. At worst, they'd lose the deposit and first month's rent, but she was right that there were other places.

In the morning, Grant called in sick and packed up some more odds and ends and loaded up his truck. He got a storage building and loaded it up with boxes. Finally, on Friday, he took the keys and a note to Mr. Herbert's office. Mr. Herbert was on the golf course, so his secretary just took the big brown envelope and jotted down that the Wylies had changed their minds and decided to let the ghosts have their house back.

ABOUT THE AUTHOR

TALLY JOHNSON is a graduate of Spartanburg Methodist College and Wofford College with degrees in history. He is the author of *Ghosts of the South Carolina Upcountry, Ghosts of the South Carolina Midlands, Ghosts of the Pee Dee* (all for The History Press) and *Civil War Ghosts of South Carolina* (for Post Mortem Press) and has a story in *An Improbable Truth: The Paranormal Adventures of Sherlock Holmes* (from Mocha Memoirs Press) as well as two stories in *44 Lies by 22 Authors* (for Post Mortem Press). He is the winner of the Appreciation Award from the 2017 USC-Union Upcountry Literary Festival.

Mr. Johnson currently serves as Special Services Coordinator for the Chester County Library in Chester SC. He is on the South Carolina Arts Council's Roster of Approved Artists as an author, as well as the South Carolina School Librarians' list of storytellers. Tally is also the permanent Storyteller in Residence for the Palmetto State Hangers hammock camping group. He enjoys spending time with his family and friends, hiking, hammock camping, visiting historic sites, and reading. He has been a guest at ConGregate, ConCarolinas, Fandom Fest, MonsterCon, MystiCon, AtomaCon, and Imaginarium.

Made in the USA
Middletown, DE
07 May 2022

65444935R00097